J.H. Riddell

Phemie Keller

Vol. 1

J.H. Riddell

Phemie Keller
Vol. 1

ISBN/EAN: 9783337346560

Printed in Europe, USA, Canada, Australia, Japan

Cover: Foto ©Andreas Hilbeck / pixelio.de

More available books at **www.hansebooks.com**

PHEMIE KELLER.

A Novel.

By F. G. TRAFFORD,

AUTHOR OF "GEORGE GEITH," "CITY AND SUBURB," "MAXWELL DREWITT,"
"TOO MUCH ALONE," "WORLD AND THE CHURCH," "RACE FOR WEALTH."

IN THREE VOLUMES.
VOL. I.

LONDON:
TINSLEY BROTHERS, 18, CATHERINE ST., STRAND.
1866.

LONDON:
BRADBURY, EVANS, AND CO., PRINTERS, WHITEFRIARS.

CONTENTS.

CONTENTS.

PHEMIE KELLER.

CHAPTER I.

AMONG THE ⟨ ⟩LS.

HE had been toiling under the noontide heat
up the narrow defile which led from Grassenfel
to Tordale. He had grown weary of the way, of
the rough path, of the rugged scenery. He had
looked to his right hand and to his left, and
behold on the one side stormy Skillanscar met
his view, whilst on the other the peaks of Helbeck rose towering to the summer sky.

He had looked straightforward, and there were
mountains still—mountains that seemed to hem
him in, and make him a prisoner in their rocky
fastnesses.

Toiling onward, he had been thinking how long
was the road ; how great the distance ; when all

at once the path bore sharply round the base of a projecting rock, and brought him suddenly within view of Tordale Church.

With the everlasting hills overshadowing it, with the murmuring waterfall singing ever and. always beside it; the sweet melody to which so few came to listen—with the larches and the pines waving their branches gently over the grassy mounds 'in the graveyard, with the August sun pouring his beams down the mountains on the dancing rivulet, on the smooth velvety turf, Tordale Church stood on a little mound commanding a view of the valley, that broke like a revelation of beauty on the traveller.

He had walked far to see this piece of God's handiwork ; he had toiled wearily up the defile, over the rocks, between the mountains, to find this gem which was set so securely among the hills, that the eye of stranger rarely rested on it.   He had walked far, and he felt that he was not so young as formerly ; yet when the glorious view opened before him Captain Henry Gower Stondon forgot the distance, thought no longer of fatigue, but, pausing, drank in the loveliness he beheld.

It was high noon among the Cumberland hills —high noon on a Sunday in August—and the mighty Sabbath hush pervaded all Nature, whether animate or inanimate.

Far away down the valley, where the rivulet trickled on slowly to join the Derwent, where the grass was greenest, and the sun least scorching, cows lay lazily chewing the cud—sheep browsed the sweet herbage leisurely. There was a solemn stillness amongst the mountains; the sunbeams rested in great patches where they had first fallen; the wind, as it came and went, and went and came, stole through the tree-tops noiselessly; no bird burst from the ivy or the broom, breaking with sudden flight the stillness of that noontide hour; the wild bee was so deep in the foxglove's bell, that it had no time to tell of the treasures lying there. Even the grasshoppers seemed to have forgotten their song; and but for the church and the graves, the stranger who now looked on Tordale for the first time, might almost have fancied that he had reached an uninhabited Eden, never before trodden by the foot of man.

Very slowly he ascended the steps leading to the graveyard—primitive steps they were, too, Captain Stondon noticed, cut out of the clay,—with a piece of the stem of a fir-tree, split in two, placed as a guard on each,—awkward and dangerous steps for unaccustomed feet to essay; but it was only well accustomed and willing feet that, as a rule, mounted them, for Tordale was far from any town, quite out of the way of tourists, and the men and the women who paced along the mountain sides, and up the valley to the church beside the waterfall, came not for any fashion's sake, not to listen to strange words and strange doctrines, but for love of the old story that will be ever fresh to each succeeding generation, as it was to the shepherds who first heard the glad tidings of great joy.

"It all comes to this at last," thought the stranger, as he sat him down in the church porch, and looked at the green mounds, at the few mossy headstones, at the one solitary attempt at a monument; "it all comes to this. Let us start where we will, let us go where we may, let us wander over the world where we like, we must end here at last; we must come to the inexorable six feet by three, to the lonesome house prepared for us before we were born. One might have thought that death would have passed over such a valley as this; that sickness could never enter here; that there were scarcely any people to die in such a nook, and yet—and yet it is just as full as its fellows; the graves are beginning to jostle one another, and new headstones are fighting for precedence with old. It is the same wherever I go; the road always ends in a churchyard, the inhabitants are always to be found here."

And with a not unpleasing feeling of melancholy, the man who thought this, let his eyes wander out, out, over the landscape on which the sleepers around could never look more.

What did the thought signify to him; what did death mean to this man who had faced it so often that it had no terrors left? What was the meaning of the reflection that passed through his mind as he sat in the church-porch, looking down upon Tordale Valley? Simply this, that though he knew in an abstract kind of way he must die, yet that the wandering life he had led, had made the idea of when, and how, and where he should meet his fate so very vague and shadowy, that he never brought the subject really home to himself, never realised that six feet by three would some day suffice him as surely as it now sufficed others who had wandered, perhaps, as far as he. After looking on all manner of cemeteries; after seeing his comrades lying down to rest in India; after visiting the sepulchres in the East; after criticising Père-la-Chaise; after passing the London pest-grounds; after treading over pavements beneath which generations slumbered peacefully; after entering country churchyards where, after life's fitful fever—after its mad delirium, after its success, its disappointments, its joys, its sorrows, its wild hopes, its unutterable agony—men and women slept that sleep, of the mysteries whereof we know so little, but which we may humbly hope is dreamless—he had come to think of death as a thing outside himself, as a fact which concerned others more than it did him.

The rude forefathers of this hamlet knew where their mortal remains would be laid. It was a hundred to one against their bodies being carried out of the valley—even so far as Grassenfel.

Most probably, as they came Sunday after Sunday to service, their eyes rested on the spot where, when they had held the plough for the last time, when they had turned their last furrow, scattered their last seed—reaped their last harvest—sold their last crops—they would be carried, as their fathers before them had been carried, and laid down far away in the earth, beyond the cold of the winter snows, beyond the heat of the summer sun, out of the sight of the young spring flowers—where the moaning of the autumn winds and the rustle of the autumn leaves might never disturb their repose.

"How close all this must bring death," thought the traveller. "What a certainty they must feel about it—what a strange feeling such people must have on the subject." And Captain Henry

Gower Stondon grew so interested in the idea that he leaned his chin on his hand preparatory to thinking out the matter with greater comfort.

"It must bring it very near. I do not know that I should like it;" and then he went on to reflect further that it must be unpleasant also to have the whole of life bounded by those hills, by those frowning mountains; to have to play out the whole drama of existence in that green sequestered valley; to have the horizon of external experience brought so near that an hour's walk at any time would enable a man to lay his hand upon it; to have his internal hopes, wishes, fears, joys, bound up in a few acres of land, in a score or so of acquaintances; to have Grassenfel for his longest excursion; to see those eternal peaks for ever lifting their heads to the sky; to come Sunday after Sunday through the valley, up the steps, across the threshold, and so into the little church, in the porch of which he was then sitting; to be christened there; to be married there; to be buried in some nook of the graveyard that sloped so sunnily towards the south! Captain

Stondon, who had been a wanderer on the face of the earth from his youth up, decided that he should not like such a lot at all; and that such a lot—the sole birthright of millions—was a curious one to sit in the shade and strive to realise.

From the porch he could get a side view into the church; he could see some of the people about whom he was speculating—a fine stalwart race of men and women—a generation of handsome giants, with faces hard and steady and impassive, and enduring as the mountains under whose shadow they dwelt. A people who had something of the Scotch blood in them, who were not a fickle and light-minded generation, but rather occasionally be a trifle obstinate and stiffnecked.

Their very psalms were not as the spiritual songs of the dwellers in cities, of the inhabitants of the plains. There was a fierceness about the old Cameronian hymn they were singing which seemed in keeping with the loneliness, the desolation, the unutterable grandeur and solitude of the spot wherein this isolated band praised the Lord.

There was no organ—a violin and a flute sufficed to guide the choir; and with all their hearts, and with all their souls, the congregation aided the vocalists. The singing might be a little loud, perhaps, but it was not discordant; and suddenly, at the third verse, as though she had been holding back till the others got so thoroughly into the air as to overlook her, some girl lifted up her young, clear voice; and while Captain Stondon almost involuntarily rose to listen, mourned out,—

" Our night is dreary, and dim is our day,
And if Thou shalt turn Thy face away,
We are sinful, feeble, and helpless dust,
With none to look to, and none to trust."

" What a voice!—good Heavens, what a voice!" thought the officer; and he drew more to the inner door to see if he could discover the singer.

A chord or two from the violin, and the hymn proceeded,—

" The powers of darkness are all abroad,
They know no Saviour, they fear no God;
And we are trembling in dumb dismay—
Oh, turn not Thou Thy face away!"

He had entered the church by this time, and found her. She was but three seats from the porch. He could have stretched out his arm and touched her; but the sexton, honest old man, just as though he divined the stranger's wishes, opened the door of the pew she alone occupied, and signed to Captain Stondon to enter, which signal Captain Stondon, nothing loth, obeyed accordingly, and with his face bent over his hat, hearkened to the last verse,—

> " Thine aid, O mighty One, we crave,
> Not shortenèd is Thine arm to save;
> Let not Thine anger ever burn—
> Return, O Lord of Hosts, return ! "

Then the officer, who, though he might be as polite as most people, was not above feeling human curiosity, turned and looked at the girl, who owned a voice which seemed to him more like the warbling of a bird than anything he had ever heard before in his life,—turned and looked at Phemie Keller, at a girl dressed in a pink muslin gown, which had evidently been bought and made for some middle-aged woman, which had been as evidently worn shabby by the older individual, and cut down and altered for its present wearer—a divinity in a washed-out, large-patterned curiously befrilled dress, a Hebe in a cottage bonnet trimmed with brown and white checked ribbons — a beauty who wore thread gloves, and had on a rusty-black silk cape that might have belonged to Noah's grandmother.

But her face ! Such perfection of colour—such delicacy of feature ! Where had this rustic stolen her beauty ? Eyes of the deepest, softest, darkest blue ; eyes that looked black when you looked at them in the shade ; dark brows and lashes ; and hair—without half a dozen paints to my hand to mix together, and blend, and powder with gold dust, I could never hope to show what Phemie's hair was like ; and I could not then, because, as she moved, the shade changed also. Now it was sunny, now brown, now red, now brown and sunny, now red and brown ; and then red, and gold, and brown, would all mix and shimmer together in the varying light.

Hair to have made one of the old Venetian painters go mad, first with rapture and then with anger, because brush and palette could never hope to reproduce its colouring—hair that might well (to recall the quaint conceit of other days) tangle a lover in its meshes;—hair such as Captain Stondon had never seen before, though he had mixed much with society, and been favoured with locks, not a few, in the days when he was young, in the days that were gone and fled.

In the matter of beauty, the officer had, his whole life long, been possessed of a truly catholic taste. Before loveliness he had always, figuratively speaking, bared his head, and bowed down and worshipped. Dark locks and shining curls, sorrowful eyes, dimpled cheeks, laughing girls, thoughtful women, tall and stately, short and fairylike, Captain Stondon had admired them all. Given a woman, and pretty, and he would kneel at any shrine. He would pay compliments, he would flatter, he would lay all good gifts at the feet of his divinity save love, and that in the years departed he had given once to one woman, and could offer no more, as he firmly believed, to any living being.

That one woman had won his heart, worn it,

played with it, exhibited it, and then, weary of the toy, had flung it under foot, and trampled it in her wicked selfishness, in her unfeeling triumph.

She sold herself for money, for the pomps and vanities of a world which courted her exceedingly, and went and stayed at her house, and followed her to the grave, and then strove, not without success, to console her husband for her loss. She had deserted the poor man for the rich; but though she had used the former despitefully, though she had made him work hard for her sake, though she had left his early manhood and middle age lonely, he had been true to the love of his youth, and loved no woman since.

He had admired, he had followed in the train of many a queen of beauty, he had whispered soft nothings, he had flirted, perhaps, but he had not loved, he had not married. Matchmakers had given him up in despair; manœuvring mammas valued Captain Stondon's opinion of their daughters, simply because it was the opinion of a connoisseur, not because it was that of a person who might be expected to take any shares in the matrimonial market. He knew what was what, in a word, and he consequently knew that the young girl with the divine voice would grow up into a most beautiful woman.

"Well dressed," thought the officer, critically examining her, while the clergyman adjusted his spectacles, and opened his sermon-case, and coughed, and looked for his pocket-handkerchief, —"well dressed, well instructed, with a clever chaperone, what a sensation she would make in a West End drawing-room! What a pity that she should have been born to wear her grandmother's old gowns in a place like this, for ——"

"For the wages of sin is death," was the text that terminated both his scrutiny and his soliloquy; and if Captain Stondon had thought for a moment that the young lady might be conscious at once of her own beauty and of his admiration, he was immediately undeceived by her handing him her open Bible, his attention being called to the passage in question by the finger of Miss Keller's well-worn glove.

It was a shock; it tried the officer's gravity for

the moment; but his companion so evidently
regarded him as a very common-place stranger,
to whom she was nevertheless bound to offer the
customary civility of the neighbourhood, that it
would have been difficult for him to help feeling
his vanity touched also.

Nevertheless, he took the book, and he looked
at the text, and he listened to the sermon, not a
bad one by the way, with the attention expected
from him ; and, when the service was over, he
walked out into the graveyard, where, taking
possession of a quiet corner, he watched the congregation returning, some down the valley, some
under the shadow of the mountains, some up the
hill paths, to their respective homes.

If there were one figure the officer's eyes followed longest, it was that of the girl beside whom
he sat in church. She had waited for a man
whom Captain Stondon recognised as the violinist
of the choir, and he now looked after the pair as
they climbed the side of Helbeck, and wended
their way—whither ?

Listening to the low murmur of the waterfall—

looking idly now down the valley, now up to the summit of the distant hills—Captain Stondon stood with his arms resting on the churchyard wall, cogitating whether he should return to Grassenfel, or inquire for some place near at hand in which to rest and refresh himself, when he was roused from his reverie by the clergyman, who, passing through the graveyard, saw the stranger, and spoke to him.

The place was so lonely—so few tourists penetrated to Tordale—that it seemed natural to the clergyman to accost the middle-aged individual who had listened with much apparent attention to his sermon.

Where people are few acquaintanceship is easy. Perhaps also the clergyman saw something in the bearing of the stranger which had been overlooked by Miss Keller; in any case, he paused to speak, and then the two men walked down the steps side by side, and, turning from the direct path, strolled towards the waterfall together.

It was a picturesque spot: over the rock came the mountain stream, dropping with a dull, mono-

tonous splash into the basin it had worn for itself
below, whence over moss-grown stones it trickled
off into the valley beyond. A few trees over-
shadowed the pool beside which Captain Stondon
and his companion stood for a moment in silence
looking at the Fall; ivy and lichens covered the
face of the rocks, ferns and foxgloves grew
between the stones, and the water bathed the
green banks, and touched the familiar flowers,
and mosses, and blades of grass caressingly, ere it
left them behind for ever.

There were broom and gorse, and patches of
heather on the hill-side; underfoot, the turf was
smooth as velvet; above their heads was the
clear blue sky; around was loneliness and nature;
and, as if reluctant to break the spell, the two
men held their peace, until Captain Stondon,
stepping from stone to stone in order to reach the
basin, declared he must have a draught of the
water, it looked so cool, and pure, and sparkling.

"While you drink you should wish," remarked
the clergyman, with a smile; "and if it be, as I

suppose, your first draught, your desire will surely be gratified."

" Wish!" repeated the other, seating himself on a fragment of rock. " It is an important moment. What shall I wish ? "

" You must not tell me, or wishing will be useless," was the reply.

" What have I to wish for ? " persisted the officer; "what is there left that I could wish to come to pass, unless for the years of my youth to be given back to me ? and I could scarcely wish for that. Mine has been a happy lot as lots go ; still, I do not know that I should like to travel the road over again."

" Can you wish nothing for your wife ? "

" I have none. I have neither wife nor child, sister nor brother, nephew nor niece," and as he said this a change came over his face, and, stooping towards the pool, he took a long, deep draught, as he did so silently wishing this wish, or rather praying this prayer, " O God, when Thy good time comes, leave me not to die alone !"

Then he stepped back on to the green turf, and

the pair fell into conversation about the place and its scenery, about the parish and its inhabitants, about the church, and how long it had been built, about Cumberland generally, and finally about the world that, full of temptation and struggle and pleasure and disappointment, lay outside those mountains, far away from the green valley of Tordale.

CHAPTER II.

TORDALE.

IT was so seldom that the Vicar of Tordale met with any man able and willing to talk about the outside world in which he had once played his part, that he felt loth to lose his new acquaintance, and insisted on Captain Stondon accompanying him home, and acceping of such hospitality as a widower's *ménage* could afford.

Finding the prospect of rest and refreshment by no means disagreeable, the officer availed himself of the invitation, and before the afternoon was ended, very friendly relations were established between himself and his host.

Both were lonely men; but there all similarity between themselves or their antecedents stopped. The one had lost; the other had never possessed.

The one had hoped much, and yet the low-ceiled parlour of a country vicarage, which a stranger rarely entered, to which there came few new books, no excitement, no change, sufficed him now; the other had started in life with his way to make, with no apparent future save what his own right arm should win for him, and yet at forty-five he came back from India to enter into possession of Marshland Manor and four thousand a year.

The vicar had married young, and been the father of many children; the officer had never married, and at fifty-six had no nearer relative than Montague Stondon, barrister-at-law, who was some fifteenth cousin of the owner of Marshlands, and next heir to that desirable property and the rents appertaining thereto.

Captain Stondon had done his best for his relative; he had invited him to Marshlands; he sent him up presents of game and fruit and—money; he paid for the education of Montague Stondon's only son; and the thanks he got for all his kindness was a morning and evening aspiration which the barrister never failed to utter for his speedy translation to a better world.

Montague Stondon would have driven his relative into matrimony years before, had it not been for that little romantic corner of his heart, wherein he had placed his young ideal of what marriage should be—an ideal from which the world and its ways had never estranged him; and so it was quite a settled matter with everybody who knew anything about the property that Captain Stondon would never have chick nor child, and that if Montague Stondon outlived his cousin, he might confidently expect to enter into possession of the Norfolk estates, which were, by the way, strictly entailed.

Without domestic ties, without household treasures, it was natural that Captain Stondon should reside but little in Norfolk—that he should remain indeed only for a very short period in any place.

During the ten years that had elapsed since his return from India he had visited many countries, seen many and many a foreign town. His pass-

ports would have bound up into quite a bulky
volume; and whenever he started on a fresh pilgrimage, Montague Stondon offered up his little
litany for him to be brought back to England a
corpse.

It might be excusable, and very probably was
excessively natural; but still nobody could say
it was pleasant for a man to know, as Captain
Stondon knew perfectly well, that his cousin,
limping with bleeding feet along the flinty road to
ruin, was cursing him for wearing good shoes and
declining to take them off for his benefit.

Wherever he went, Captain Stondon felt that
he had his cousin's best wishes for some misadventure to befall him; and as he sat opposite to
the clergyman, and listened to his tale of how
this boy had been drowned, of how that one had
studied too hard to pass his examination, and died
three weeks afterwards of brain-fever; of how his
only daughter had married happily, only to be
laid a twelvemonth afterwards in her coffin with
her baby on her breast—he thought that after all
it might be better to have these memories than

none at all—to have loved and lost, rather than never to have had anything on earth to take home and love and entreat the Lord to spare.

For these children were with the vicar still; their memories were green in his heart, and would remain there till he went to join them; and it seemed preferable to endure much misery rather than know no happiness; to bear partings on earth, to the end that some friends might be waiting to greet the wayfarer when he reached the eternal shores.

To the vicar his children were not dead—they slept; they were not lost—merely gone before.

"He had one boy in India," he said; and Captain Stondon at once inquired in what part.

"Benares—he is buried there," explained the clergyman, and he covered his face with his hands for a moment, before he went on to tell how his son had gone out to India full of youth, and hope, and life—to die.

By degrees, when he had exhausted the tale of his troubles, Mr. Conbyr grew quite cheerful, and

talked at large of his parishioners, their peculiarities, their prejudices, their attachments. Like
all clergymen, he had his little budget of petty
annoyances to open and explain—how there was a
strong element of Dissent in Tordale ; how Metho-
dists from Grassenfel held house-to-house meet-
ings ; how the service was not conducted exactly
to his liking'; how he wanted a new collection of
psalms, and his congregation would have none of
it ; how the choir was poor, and required an organ
to back it ; how sorely Tordale stood in need of a
squire and squire's family to take a high hand in
the parish ; and how, in fact, Tordale required but
being altered in every particular to become a
model valley—a valley for all England to hear of
and envy.

Then he retraced his steps, and praised his
people, their sturdy independence, their rough-
and-ready kindness, their thorough devotion, their
willingness to help one another ; and how long he
would have gone on lauding their virtues it is
impossible to say, had Captain Stondon, seizing
his opportunity, not inquired,—

" Pray what is the name of that young person who was in the same pew with me to-day—a girl with auburn hair, and a magnificent voice ? "

" Oh ! you remarked her voice, did you ? That is the cousin, or niece, or niece by marriage, or something, of the very singular individual who plays the violin in church. · She is called Phemie Keller—sings sweetly, I consider, and is pretty, too. Do you not think so ? "

" Sings sweetly ! What can the man be made of," thought Captain Stondon, " to use such an expression about the matter ? Sings sweetly ! If the nightingale came outside his bedroom window and trilled to him all the night long, he would get up in the morning and say he had heard a nice bird whistling. Pretty, too ! " Straightway the officer fell to wondering what manner of woman the deceased Mrs. Conbyr had been—whether she had black hair as coarse as a horse's mane, and a Roman nose, high cheek-bones, and hard eyes ; or whether she was a washed-out looking creature, with the pink of her face running into the white, and sandy-

coloured corkscrew curls, and an anxious, frightened expression of countenance.

He thought a person who called Miss Keller
only pretty must have very benighted ideas on
the subject of beauty; and yet the fact was, Mr.
Conbyr had married quite a belle, a sparkling
brunette, whose friends all thought she threw herself away when she accepted a curate with only a
prospective living for his fortune.

Mrs. Conbyr had been a toast, a flirt, a very
captivating, winning little creature, and perhaps
it was no wonder that now she was dead, her
husband held to her memory as to his beau-ideal
of all which was most lovely and charming in
woman. Nevertheless even he admitted that Miss
Keller was pretty.

"And intelligent, too," he added; "if she
wouldn't giggle so much, and hadn't such stuck-
up ideas, and would dress herself more like a
farmer's niece, she might grow into a superior
woman. But vanity is the besetting sin of the
whole household. Aggland himself tells you can-
didly he considers he understands the violin better·

than any man in the country, and he calls his brother farmers, openly, fools and prejudiced donkeys. As for me, he thinks me perfectly ignorant of theology. He has a curious smattering of learning; can talk French a little, German a little, and quote some Latin passages. He draws likewise, and formerly used to play on the guitar. He has begun to build himself an organ, which he offered to present to the church when completed, if I would give him the sole management of the choir. He had laid himself out to have none but the members of his own family in it, and depended on Phemie to lead; but she refused, and saved me the trouble and annoyance of declining. 'Ah, there is the cloven foot peeping out,' he said, as if delivering an oration; 'the taint of aristocracy, which hates to do anything for the democracy, appearing.'"

"And what the deuce did he mean?" asked Captain Stondon, bewildered.

"Why, he meant, I suppose, that she didn't care to sing, and that there was good blood in her veins. I fancy she is illegitimate. He is always

raving against the better classes—quite a character, I assure you."

" Do your mountains grow many such ? " asked
his guest.

" He is not a home product," was the reply.
" Erratic genius of that description is not indige-
nous to the Cumberland soil. He is from Here-
ford, and his present wife is Lancashire, and his
niece Scotch. His first wife was Scotch also, I
fancy, and he has a tribe of young Agglands,
sturdy, independent children of the hills. It is a
strange household altogether, and one that, could
I persuade you to stay with me, I should take you
to see."

" Thank you," said Captain Stondon; "but I must
leave Cumberland to-morrow. I am going first to
Norfolk, and then abroad. I shall always think
pleasantly," he added, after a pause, " of the valley
of Tordale ; always retain a memory of the happy
Sunday afternoon I have spent with you." And
with that, as it was now getting on towards the
hour for evening service, and as he had far to
walk before he could reach Grassenfel and his inn

together, the officer rose to go, but his intention was overruled by his host.

"I will not ask you," he said, "to come to church, because, if you must return to Grassenfel to-night, it would throw you too late on the road; but walk back with me to the waterfall, and then I will show you a path which runs right along the side of Helbeck for a couple of miles at least. You can form no idea of the beauty and grandeur of the defile till you have seen it from above, and the path, an easy one, leads down to the road you came by before you reach the Broken Stone bridge. The view from the top is worth seeing. I only wish this was Monday instead of Sunday, so that I could go with you myself."

Having made which frank confession the clergyman looked out his sermon, put on his hat, took his stick, and announced his readiness to depart.

"I can accompany you a little way up the path," he said; and accordingly the pair sallied out again together, and sauntered through the green vale side by side.

If Tordale had looked lovely in the noon time, it was more beautiful still in the soft evening light. It wanted then nearly an hour to sunset, but the western sky was already like molten gold. Down the hill-sides long shadows were lying; still, sad, and stern looked the mountain peaks, with each jagged projection—each sharp outline—clearly reflected against the evening sky. A cloud frowned over Helbeck, which betokened a storm, the clergyman thought.

" But it is scarcely warm enough for thunder," he added; "and unless the wind die away we shall not have any rain before morning. Is not our valley lovely, Captain Stondon? When you are abroad—when you are looking at what is considered ·far more magnificent scenery,—will you ever think, I wonder, of our little nook hidden away among the Cumberland hills?"

" I shall never forget Tordale," answered the officer, truthfully enough; but little knowing how truthfully, for all that.

In the after days of joy and of sorrow which he was then walking on, to pass through to reach

the end, he forgot the name of many a town—
he forgot the road by which he had travelled to
many a city; mountain passes, smiling lakes, the
weariness of Indian marches, gorgeous Eastern
palaces, the brilliancy of Eastern flowers—these
things were forgotten, or remembered only as a
man remembers dreams. The Hindoo standing
by his sacred river, the Arabs in the desert, the
long line of foam that alone broke the eternity
of waters as the outward-bound ship cleft her
way to the Cape, the tramp of the sailors as they
paced the deck, the faces of his old comrades
faded, as the years stole on out of sight and out
of mind; but clear and distinct, like the memory
of his mother's face—like the recollection of his
boyhood's home—Tordale stood out a picture hung
on the walls of his heart for ever.

He was never to forget it—never to forget the
glory of its noontide, the murmur of its waterfall, the calm of its lonely graveyard, the ivy, the
ferns, the foxglove and the broom. In the loneliness and solitude of night he was to feel the
calm of that scene soothe his spirit once again.

He had but to close his eyes, and he could hear the dull plash of the waterfall, the rustling of the leaves, the mourning farewell of the rivulet. He could look at the long wet blades of grass bending ever and always into the water, and turning down the stream as though wanting to be pulled from their roots, that they might float away and away with the brook, first to the river and then to the sea. He could hear the water trickling among the stones; he could touch the moss with his powerless fingers; he could feel the cool drops touching his parched lips; he could remember how he had drained a deep draught from the basin in the rock; and then he would think likewise, if he hasted not to exorcise the evil thought, of his unavailing petition, of the prayer which had been granted to the letter, not in the spirit, to add to his troubles rather than to increase his joy.

CHAPTER III.

IN DANGER.

AFTER parting from his new friend, Captain Stondon ascended the path that led past the waterfall, across the little mountain stream, and half way to the top of Helbeck. It was hard work climbing up the track which wound now through rocks, now over stones, till skirting the side of the mountain it bore off straight towards Grassenfel.

Heather, purple and glowing, bordered the track—wild flowers grew beside it. The whole earth was tinted with the hues of August. The richest, the most luxuriant month of all the year was sweeping, like a king in his glory, over the hills and the valleys, decking the former in their robes of state, clothing the latter with the yellow of the ripening corn and the emerald of the aftermath. To the right lay Tordale, bathed in the beams of the setting sun; below him lay the defile that led to Grassenfel; and, like a speck, he could discern the Broken Bridge which he must cross on his way back to his inn. Every crag and peak of Skillanscar shone in the bright rays of the glory wherein the whole landscape was steeped; and Captain Stondon, who had sat himself down amongst the heather to watch to its close this sunset amid the mountains, acknowledged to his heart that he had never seen anything in the way of scenery which so thoroughly satisfied and filled his soul as the smiling valley and the desolate hills—the gloomy ravine and the grey rugged mountains, on all of which the sun poured his light as though he were blessing the green earth ere leaving her to darkness and repose.

At last, with more than his accustomed pomp of red and gold and purple, he set behind the hills; and, as he did so, the cloud Mr. Conbyr had noticed, rolled up from the east, covering Helbeck with a dark curtain of gloom. It was very grand to see Skillanscar reflecting back the glory of the western sky, but it was by no means agreeable to Captain Stondon to perceive a storm brewing so near him. He knew he had lingered too long on the road already; for which reason he quickened his pace, and hurried to reach the point where the path began to descend into the ravine below. If he could but get to the Broken Stone bridge before the rain began, he thought he should be better able to work his way to Grassenfel.

It was not easy, however, to walk fast along the narrow track he was following, and when he at length commenced to descend, a flash of lightning heralded the approach of the coming storm. If his life had depended on it, Captain Stondon could not have helped halting to listen for the first peal of the thunder. After a pause it came, breaking the silence at first with a sullen roar like that of a distant cannonade; but with every flash it drew nearer and nearer, echoing from mountain to mountain, from summit to summit, till one might almost have thought that height was defying height, and firing volley after volley across the defile.

With the sun the wind had sunk to rest likewise, and as he stood watching the lightning darting down the hill-sides, running along the rocks, and leaping from crag to crag like a living foe, Captain Stondon became conscious that the air had suddenly become warm and oppressive, and that a heat like that of a furnace seemed to pervade the atmosphere.

"What an idiot I was to come this way at all," he thought; "what a still greater idiot to loiter as I have done." And with the lightning racing past him, with the thunder crashing and roaring overhead, the officer turned his face steadily towards the defile and pursued his road downwards.

But spite of all his haste he got on but slowly. In places the descent was steep and the path slippery; wherever grass grew, or wherever rock and stone mixed with the earth, it was difficult to get a firm footing. What with the evening shadows which were beginning to fall, and the dark-

ness of the cloud overhead, and the dazzling
flashes of the lightning that made everything
seem darker afterwards for their sudden brilliancy,
he soon found he was feeling his way rather than
seeing it—groping down the path rather than
pacing it securely.

"If I could but reach the road in the ravine,"
he muttered, as he slipped and staggered and
recovered himself, and then slipped again. "If I
were only safe at the bottom I might——"

He never completed that mental sentence, for
at the instant he stumbled over a loose stone and
rolled down the path, clutching as he went
at the short grass, at the heather, at the
brambles.

Fighting for dear life, he caught sticks and
stones; he tried to save himself by grasping the
very earth itself; he saw as he went over and
over, the mountain peaks, the ravine, the road he
had been trying to reach, the track by which he
had descended. He could see at that moment as
he could not have seen had he been standing
erect, with the noontide sun shining upon him.

Even in his struggle he found time to wonder what would stop him—whether he should be dashed to pieces ? Among the mountain peaks— a hundred miles above him as it seemed—the thunder was pealing. He heard it as he had heard the roaring of cannon on battle-fields far away. The lightning came flashing down among the rocks, and he found time to remember it resembled the flash which followed " Fire !" in the days when he was fighting like the best; and then all at once he held out his arms instinctively to save himself, and with a crash his descent was arrested ; and stunned, and bruised, and battered —he remembered no more.

When he came to his senses it was dark, and the rain pouring in torrents ; the lightning had ceased ; the thunder had rolled far away ; there was not a sound to be heard save the rushing of the rain, and the greedy noise which the dry earth made as she drank the welcome moisture in. It was some time before he could remember what had happened, and then he tried to raise himself, but fell back shrieking with pain.

He shouted for help, but if help had been close at hand, the noise of the pelting rain sweeping down the mountains would have drowned his feeble cries. Mercilessly, pitilessly the rain beat upon him as he lay there powerless. With an effort he turned his face towards the piece of rock which had stayed his fall; and while the large drops fell on his unprotected head, he lay and thought in a kind of half delirium about the end that was to be.

Was he to die there? Was he to die all alone on the mountain side with the rain pouring down upon him, alone in this solitude, amid the darkness of night? Before now he had lain wounded on a battle-field, but that had not seemed so desolate as this. His comrades had sought him out then, but here no one would dream of looking for him. His landlord at Grassenfel did not know where he had gone; he had no one to miss him—to wonder at his absence; no one in Cumberland —no one on earth.

If Montague Stondon could only imagine where he was lying, how happy he would be. Was he to die thus to gratify him? Was the life-story (one which had been none too happy) to be finished thus? How long could he lie there and live? Was it likely any one would find him? Would his body ever be discovered, or would it lie there for the winter's snows to fall on?—for the winter's wind to moan over?

If he was not found, how soon could Montague Stondon take possession of Marshlands? Was there any chance of making himself heard? How far down the ravine did he lie? When the morning dawned he should be able to see. His arm was broken, he supposed, but the intolerable pain in his ankle was harder to endure than that. He tried once again to raise himself, and, spite of what the effort cost, managed to get his back up against the rock. He was drenched with rain; a pool had formed round about where he lay; every thread of his light summer clothes was saturated; and yet, though he was shivering with the damp and the wet, the pain caused by the slightest movement threw him into a violent heat.

He had not strength to keep himself against

the rock, and ere long he slipped back on to the earth,—back with a jar which made him scream aloud once more. Then everything grew confused —he was in India—he was at sea—he was at home, dreaming of being in some awful peril; he peopled the mountain sides with shapes of horror; the darkness did not seem like darkness, for he could see phantoms and spectres flitting hither and thither ceaselessly. At last they all came rushing down on him, but the very horror of the vision made him recall his scattered senses. Where was he? What had happened? He remembered, and then his mind wandered off afresh. He was a boy again, robbing the first bird's nest he had ever despoiled; he was playing truant, and looking for blackberries with Bob Sedgemore, and as they passed Farmer Gooday's straw-yard they hunted Mrs. Gooday's favourite cat with Bob's terrier up the bank of the little stream, till the poor thing turned on her tormentors, when Bob and he stoned her to death.

He had not thought about that tortoise-shell cat for seven-and-forty years. What could make him remember her now? The way she stretched out her legs and turned up her eyes was horrid, and yet Bob and he had not been affected by the sight then. Bob merely kicked her into the stream, after which agreeable interlude they went on, and ate more blackberries.

Bob was dead. He had seen his corpse so blackened with powder, so maimed, and mangled, and mutilated, that the mother who bore him would not have recognised her boy. He was dead —everybody was dead; the girl he had been walking with only the other day, as it seemed, beside the yew-hedge in her father's garden, was dead and buried too. People came by their deaths in every conceivable way, and why should he not come to his on the side of a Cumberland mountain, with the wet earth for his bed, and the rain and darkness for companions?

Heavens, how the rain poured down!—how the dead gathered round about him! There were the men and women of the long and long ago walking along the path he had followed from Tordale. He saw them looking down at him through the night. There was his mother; could she be looking for him? Yes; he could hear her light footfall on the grass—she was coming to fetch him. She put her cold hand on his cheek, and Captain Stondon, with a shout for help, fainted again.

After that he heard, as in a confused dream, answering shouts coming up the valley; he heard dogs barking, and people talking, and knew that he was lifted and carried a long distance to a house, into which he was borne like a dead man.

He remembered a vain attempt that was made to get him to swallow something which they held to his lips. He recollected subsequently the scared look with which the bystanders started back at the scream he uttered when an attempt was made to pull off his right boot; then all became a blank; for days and days he raved incessantly; for days his life hung on a thread, and he knew nothing of the patient care, of the devoted nursing which brought him back from the Valley of the Shadow of Death to the morning and the sunshine of life and health,—from the bleak hill-side and the cold earth's breast, to such home comfort, happiness, and contentment, as through all the years of his pilgrimage he had never known.

CHAPTER IV.

PHEMIE.

AFTER many days Captain Stondon, with the fever which had prostrated him subdued, awoke from a quiet sleep, and looked as well as extreme weakness would permit about the room he occupied.

The apartment was small, clean, and scantily furnished. There were white curtains to the bed, white curtains to the latticed windows.

Without moving his head, Captain Stondon could see, over the short muslin blind, the valley of Tordale stretching away below; he beheld the mountains bounding the view, and then, remembering what he had suffered amongst those mountains, he closed his eyes again, and with a sensation of luxurious weakness, fell asleep once more.

When next he woke it was getting late in the afternoon, and between him and the window next the bed there sat a man, whose face he knew he had seen before. This man was busily engaged in cleaning a gun, and with a lazy interest Captain Stondon watched him removing the barrels, and washing the stock, and going through the other ceremonies usually performed on an occasion of the kind. As he rose to leave the room, in which there was no fire, in order that he might finish the operation in orthodox fashion over some live coals, the man glanced at the bed, and noticing that his patient's eyes were open, he laid down the gun, and, stooping over the bed, inquired how the invalid felt.

"I am better, I suppose," Captain Stondon answered, feebly. "How long?"

"A fortnight," was the reply; and straight away went Mr. Aggland to his wife.

"Beef tea, Priscilla," he commanded, "beef tea of superlative strength and in unlimited quantity. He is awake and sensible. Yes," soliloquised Mr. Aggland, "he has come back to that 'stage where every man must play a part.' What have you there? Mutton broth! Let him have some of that. I did not save him from 'Such sheets of fire, such bursts of horrid thunder, such groans of roaring wind and rain,' to let him die of starvation at last."

"Lor' a mercy, Daniel, how you do talk," remarked his better half, as she obeyed his commands. "Give you your own way, and I believe you would stew down a bullock for him."

"And why not, woman?" demanded her husband: "why not a bullock? What is the life of a beast in comparison to the life of a man; not that I myself——" At which point Mr. Aggland, growing argumentative, was interrupted by a little scream from his wife.

"For any sake, Daniel, don't turn its mouth next me! Put it down, or I won't take up the broth at all."

"Mercy alive! it has not a barrel on it. There is not a thing about it to go off. It is as harmless now as my walking-stick."

"Well, harmless or not, I can't a-bear it nigh

me," answered Mrs. Aggland. "I had just as lief see a lion in the room as a gun. How does the gentleman seem, Daniel? Has he spoken at all?"

"Yes, but I don't want him to speak much till he has eaten. What says Burns?—

> ' Food keeps us livin',
> Tho' life's a gift no worth receivin'.' "

"Drat Burns!" interposed Mrs. Aggland. "Ay, and for that matter," she continued, "drat all them poets, say I. Here, take the broth, and I'll send one of the boys over to Grassenfel in the morning to see if we can get any beef. Won't I go up to him? Not I, indeed. Am I fit, Daniel, am I fit—I put it to you—to be looked at by any gentleman? There's Phemie,—if you want anybody to go and see him, ask her. She's always dressed; she always seems just to have come out of a bandbox; she has not to go mucking about like your wife; she is a lady, and can sit in her parlour. Ask her."

"I will, my dear, as you wish it," replied Mr. Aggland, and he went straight into the apartment his wife called the parlour, but which was in reality the living room of the family, where sat the apple of discord in the Aggland household, with a pile of needlework before her that it would have appalled the most skilful seamstress to attack.

If that was being a lady, Daniel Aggland decided then, as he had decided many a time before, the position was not one to be envied. Rather the baking and brewing and cooking than that eternal stitch—stitch! And, moreover, had not Phemie to do many a thing about the house besides stitching? Whenever the bread was best and lightest, had not Phemie kneaded it? When the butter was the colour of the daffodil, had not Phemie's soft, white hands, that no work made hard or coarse, taken it off the churn? Who dressed the children, and sent them clean and tidy off to school? Phemie, to be sure. Who helped them with their lessons, and caused the three batches of children (the Agglands by the first wife, the Agglands by the second wife, and the Kings, whose mother had brought them with her to the Cumberland farm,

as her contribution to the general weal) to be
far ahead of all competitors in their respective
classes ?   Who made and mended for them all ?
Phemie. Who sewed the buttons on Mr. Aggland's
shirts, and kept his clothes in the order he loved ?
Why, Phemie still, who now sat with her lovely
hair reflecting back the sunbeams, plying her
needle busily.

She was not dressed in the finery to which Mr.
Conbyr had taken exception—finery that had
descended to her from Mrs. Aggland ; and there
was so great a contrast between her beauty and
her attire, that Mr. Aggland felt it strike him
painfully.

He loved the girl, and would have clothed her
in silks and satins if he could.   With the memory
of all that was calmest, and best, and happiest in
his life, she was interwoven ; and he would have
liked to make her lot different, if only for the
affection he had borne to the dead woman who
was so fond of her.

Further, he admired beauty, and the beautiful,
in his opinion, had no business to be useful like-

wise ; for both of which reasons Mr. Aggland, with his wife's complaints of Phemie's "uppishness" still ringing in his ears, could not help but pause and look at the girl who, if Mrs. Aggland's oft-repeated assertion might be believed, "was not worth her salt."

A really pretty woman always looks prettier without her bonnet, and Phemie Keller proved no exception to this rule. The small well-shaped head with its glory of luxuriant hair, the white graceful neck, the shell-like ear!—the bonnet had concealed all these things from Captain Stondon's eyes,—and stripped of the old-fashioned clothes which were her very best, and dressed in a faded and well-darned mousseline de laine of the smallest pattern imaginable, which de laine had likewise descended to her from remote centuries, with her soft round arms peeping from below the open sleeves, with her snowy collar fastened by a bow of dark brown ribbon, Phemie Keller sitting in the sunshine with the pile of unfinished work before her, looked every inch what she was—a lady.

"Will you carry this up to our patient, Phemie?" said her uncle; and there was a tone in his voice as he spoke which made the girl look at him wonderingly. "He is awake now—awake and sensible; but we must keep plenty of oil in the lamp, or it will go out after all our trouble."

"It won't go out, uncle, for want of oil while you are in the house," she answered, laying down her work and taking the tray from him. "Duncan had better run down to the Rectory when he comes back from school, had he not, and tell Mr. Conbyr the good news? Do you remember how, when he was at the very worst, you used to say he would do us credit yet? Arn't you proud to have saved him? I am."

That last speech, I am very sorry to say, had a spice of antagonism in it. Mrs. Aggland had said, whenever she got tired of the extra fuss and trouble, that as the man was sure to die any-way, he might better have died on the hill-side than in the house of poor folks like themselves, for which reason Phemie was triumphantly glad that Captain Stondon had lived, " if only to spite the cross old thing," the latter observation being made in strict confidence to their only servant, Peggy MacNab.

But for Mr. Aggland and Phemie it is indeed more than likely that Mrs. Aggland's prophecies might ‚have been fulfilled, and the pair had certainly cause for gratulation at the progress made by their patient.

"It is positively refreshing to see you getting on so well," remarked Mr. Aggland, as he took his seat by the bedside again, and, the broth having been swallowed, resumed his gun-cleaning performance; "but you must not talk much—you must not talk at all.   The less you exert yourself, and the more you sleep, the sooner you will be able to go—

'Chasing the wild deer and following the roe,'"

finished Mr. Aggland, who probably felt at a loss how to complete his sentence otherwise.

In compliance with this advice, Captain Stondon refrained from speaking, and did not exert himself at all, unless, indeed, looking with half-closed eyes at his host could be called exertion.

To him Mr. Aggland was a never-ending, ever-
beginning source of wonder: dark, wild-looking
hair, that looked as though it had met with some
terrible surprise, hung over a face as strange and
weird as the face of man need to be; hollow
cheeks, thoughtful, greenish-grey eyes, a large
mouth, a nose that seemed all nostril, a ragged
beard, a feeble attempt at a moustache; lines
where lines never appeared in other men's faces;
a general effect of cleverness and eccentricity.   It
was this Captain Stondon took in by degrees, as
he lay between sleeping and waking, listening to
Mr. Aggland humming, in a low falsetto,

> " The Lord my pa-hasture sha-hall prepare,
>   And feed me wihith ha she-heperd's care."

Many a day afterwards, when he saw Phemie's
gravity completely upset by her uncle's melody,
he thought how weak he must have been that
night when he first heard his host speaking in
what he called his "natural language," music.

CHAPTER V.

A COMPACT.

THERE is an Indian plant which will grow and flourish in any place, under any circumstances.

Earth it does not ask—care it does not demand. Cut it off from all apparent means of support, and it thrives notwithstanding. Detach a leaf from the parent plant, suspend it by a thread from the ceiling, and behold ! the leaf, receiving all the nourishment it requires from the atmosphere alone, puts out roots.

As he lay in bed wearily counting away the long hours of convalescence ; as he sat in the family sitting-room ; as he followed his host or his host's children slowly around the farm, Captain Stondon never ceased thinking about that strange plant, and likening it to Mr. Aggland.

Cut off apparently from all temptation to eccentricity—removed from contact with a world which,
galling sensitive natures, sometimes produces
curious mental sores and running humours in the
best—earning his bread in a primitive manner,
trying neither to his brain nor to his temper—
placed in a station that seems to have been
removed by Providence further from slight and
aggravation than any other under heaven, Mr.
Aggland was yet peculiar in his manners, habits,
and ideas,—peculiar to a degree.

Like the air plant, his oddities were self-sup-
porting and self-propagating; the older he grew,
the more eccentric he became. Time only in-
creased his prejudices; years only brought his
peculiarities into more prominent relief; a large
family merely gave him endless opportunities of
airing his pet crotchets, of exhibiting his singular
stock of information. Never by any chance did
he do anything like other people. He had a way
and a fashion of his own—even of sowing seeds in
his garden; and his ideas on the subject of train-
ing and education had produced as singular a

flock of argumentative children as could have been found in the length and breadth of "canny Cumberlan'."

True offspring of the hills—sturdy, self-reliant, self-opinionated, courageous—the Agglands and the Kings composed a remarkable household; one in which, nevertheless, whenever he was able to rise from his bed and limp about the place, Captain Stondon speedily found himself at home.

His first advances towards acquaintanceship had been received by the juvenile fry with caution, not to say suspicion. Distrust of a stranger being, however, mingled with a feeling that they held a kind of property in him, that he was the spoil of their bow and arrow, of their sword and spear, produced a certain—I cannot say graciousness— but unbending of their usual ungraciousness in his favour. They did not know what to make of this "'gowk' who had been so feckless as to miss. t' rod, and go sossing from wig to wa' down the hul;" but the very fact of their dog "Davy" having found the injured man in a "soond," and of their father having procured help and brought him home, and nursed him through his illness, caused the lads to feel a kind of compassiónate interest in their new friend.

They had been kept so much out of the sick-room that their curiosity had naturally been excited likewise. Indeed, Captain Stondon's first interview with Duncan, Mr. Aggland's eldest born, was held under difficulties, while that young gentleman stood with the chamber-door half open, surveying the man who had lain in bed till they all settled he was never going to rise again.

"Have you got anything to say to me, my lad?" asked Captain Stondon, stretching out one weak hand towards his visitor.

"No; have you got anything to say to me?" replied Duncan, clenching the handle of the door tighter as he spoke.

"I do not know that I have," answered Captain Stondon, who was rather taken aback by this unexpected question. "Did you do well at school .to-day?"

"You do not care to know that; you have no lessons to get," replied Duncan, with the air of a bird far too old to be caught by such conversational chaff, but he took a step forward into the room notwithstanding.

"Are you no dowly lying there so long?" he asked, after a pause.

"If you tell me what you mean by dowly, I will answer your question," said Captain Stondon.

"Are you thinking long? You know what that is, I suppose," explained Duncan, who had learnt the phrase from his Scotch mother.

"I am not exactly sure that I do; but if you want to know whether I am tired of being laid up here, I must answer 'yes.' I shall feel very glad to be out of bed, and walking about once more."

"I will take you to see the Strammer Tarn, if you like, when you are well," volunteered his visitor.

"Now I tell you what it is, Duncan," broke in Mr. Aggland at this juncture; "if I ever catch you here again without my permission, I will box your ears. Indeed, I have a very great mind to box them now."

And straightway the father inflicted condign punishment on his son, who retired howling from the apartment, while Mr. Aggland walked to the window, and looked out, muttering to himself, half-apologetically—

> " ' Be then to him
> As was the former tenant of your age,
> When you were in the prologue of your time,
> And he lay hid in you unconsciously,
> Under his life.' "

Captain Stondon had not the remotest idea what Mr. Aggland meant by his quotation, but he knew that the man's face looked softened and sorrowful when he turned from the window, and remarked that "boys would be boys, and that Duncan was his mother's son all over."

Of course it was impossible for Captain Stondon to negative this statement, but he thought Duncan greatly resembled his father for all that.

"You will excuse their ill-manners, sir," proceeded Mr. Aggland. "They see no one, poor things. They can learn no better in a wilderness like this. I do my best to bring them up honest men and women, 'fearing God, honouring the

'Queen.' But for anything else! What can I teach them here in this 'cell of ignorance,' as Guiderius happily calls the country."

"You can teach them what you know, doubtless," answered Captain Stondon. "Your education seems to have been much better attended to than that of most persons, whether in town or country; and you can surely impart to your children a portion at least of that which you once learnt yourself."

"Superficial—all superficial," said Mr. Aggland, with a sigh. "Here a little, there a little—a mere smattering of education. Once, indeed, the fields of learning lay open before me, but I would not when I could; and you know what is the fate of people who trifle with their opportunities. Afterwards I could not when I would; and the result is that I am here, and my children are here, and here we shall all remain till the end of the chapter. The boys, some of them, have fair abilities, and with good fortune, it is probable they may eventually——hold the plough well," finished Mr. Aggland, abruptly.

Truth was, the father had been going to end his sentence very differently, but feeling that a stranger could scarcely sympathise with his hopes, and knowing that, between the future he desired and the present in which he lived, there was a gap broad as poverty, he substituted other words for those he was about to speak, and before Captain Stondon could reply to his remark, hastened to change the subject.

"I should be sorry to go back into the world again," he said, "though I do rail at times against this wilderness, and, like Lamb, consign hills, woods, lakes, mountains, to the eternal devil. I abuse nature as men often show their tenderness by speaking disparagingly of the women they love best; and I cannot understand the state of that soul which should find its love of natural scenery satisfied by the 'patches of long waving grass and the stunted trees that blacken in the old churchyard nooks which you may yet find bordering on Thames Street.'"

"I never was in Thames Street, so far as I recollect," remarked Captain Stondon, to whom it never occurred that Mr. Aggland was quoting from a book; " but I do not think the scenery to be met with there would satisfy me. Nevertheless, I confess that for the future I shall like mountains better at a distance. Of one thing I am possitive, namely, that I shall be content hereafter to admire their beauties from below."

Mr. Aggland laughed. " You had a bad fall," he said, "and would have had a long lie of it but for Mr. Conbyr and my dog Davy. Mr. Conbyr could not rest in his bed till he had sent a man over on his Galloway to see if you were safely housed in your inn at Grassenfel; and when the news came back that you had not been heard of, nothing would serve him but that I should turn out and look for you. So Davy and I, and Jack Holms, started on the search. Mr. Combyr wanted to come with us, but I would have none of him. Davy knew what we were out for as well as if he had been a Christian."

" What breed is he?" interrupted Captain Stondon : " a St. Bernard ? "

" Not a bit of it," answered Mr. Aggland ; " he is

something between a Coolie, a Skye, and a Scotch terrier—but what I cannot tell you. Anyhow, he knew what we were looking for, and just when Jack and I thought we must give over the search, he picks up your hat, sir, and brings it to us in his teeth. Then we knew you must be somewhere in the neighbourhood, and Davy hunted about, smelling up and down till he found you behind the rock, and a nice pickle you were in when found. I had no notion but that you were dead. I tell you honestly now, sir, I no more expected ever to hear you speak when we carried you into this house, than I expect the Queen to send for me and make me an earl."

"I do not think I ever should have spoken much again but for the good care you bestowed upon me."

" Well, I flatter myself I am a tolerable nurse," replied Mr. Aggland ; " 'tis a trick I learned in my early youth. When Mr. Conbyr came here, wanting to have you carried down to the Vicarage, I said him gently nay. ' You'll excuse me, Mr. Conbyr,' I remarked, ' but out of my house the gentleman does not stir till he is fit, to make a choice for himself. You sent him up the hill-path, with a storm brewing, as any child could have told you, and I brought him off the mountain side with the rain pouring down heavens hard: so, with your leave, sir, I'll e'en see to the curing of him myself.' I suppose, however, when once you are able to limp about on a stick he will have you away, and then—'for ever and for ever farewell.' "

Here was the opening Captain Stondon had for days been anticipating, and seizing his opportunity, he assured Mr. Aggland he entertained no such passionate friendship for the clergyman as would cause him to desert the Hill Farm for the Vicarage. But at the same time Captain Stondon hinted that sickness brought its attendant expenses, that it entailed various and sundry inconveniences; that, in short, unless Mr. Aggland, who was blessed with a large family, agreed to permit the speaker, who had no children, to——"

" In short," broke in Mr. Aggland at this point, " you want to pay me; you are, I presume, rich;

I am, you presume, poor; and there you chance
to be quite correct. Whatever troubles I have,
I am not 'perk'd up in a glistering grief;' I do
not 'wear a golden sorrow.' Yes, I am a poor
man. There is no use in my trying to deny the
fact." And Mr. Aggland took a halfpenny from
his pocket, tossed it in the air, then covered it
over with his hand, and turning towards Captain Standon a little defiantly, waited for his
answer.

"I do not want to pay you," said that gentleman; "I never could pay you for the kindness
you have shown me. For my life, for the long
hours you have sat beside my bed, for all you have
done by me, I shall be your debtor always, and I
am not of so thankless a nature that I desire to
be out of your debt. All I meant was, that as
long as a man is alive you cannot keep him for
nothing—you must acknowledge the truth of that
proposition, Mr. Aggland. There is not a child
you have but costs you something every day——"

Up went the halfpenny once again, and once
again Mr. Aggland covered it with his hand.

"I, a bachelor," proceeded Captain Stondon, "should not be a burden on you, that is all. If you are willing to let me feel that I am not a burden, I will stay here, with your leave, till I am strong enough to go back to my own home ; but if not, I must try to get over to Grassenfel as soon as may be."

For the third time Mr. Aggland spun up the halfpenny. "Heads thrice running," he said, and pocketed the coin gravely.

"You have won, sir," was his answer to Captain Stondon's speech. "I *am* a poor man and money *is* an object ; but for all that, I had rather luck had turned the other way. So long as there is independence, there may be friendship even between a high man and an humble, but once money passes from hand to hand, adieu to even the semblance of equality." And with this speech Mr. Aggland would have left the room, had not Captain Stondon detained him.

"I have been a poor man myself," he said. "For years life was a continual struggle ; and those years are not so far behind me but that I can still feel more fellowship with, and friendship for, a poor man, than a rich. Because I want to be a little independent, do not think I wish to prevent your being independent likewise."

And with that he held out his hand, which Mr. Aggland took.

"Shall we be friends?" asked the officer.

"It is a question for you to decide," answered the other. "I am not a gentleman; I make no pretension to ever having been one; still—

> ' The rank is but the guinea's stamp,
> The man's the gowd for a' that.' "

And straightway it was settled that Captain Stondon should remain; that he should stay to be conducted to Strammer Tarn by Duncan; that he should wait to see Davy, the wisest dog in Cumberland; that he should not leave the Hill Farm for the Vicarage, or Grassenfel, or any other place, till he was strong and well once more; that he should not, in one word, leave Tordale till Tordale had become a part of himself—a place destined to remain green in his memory all his life long.

CHAPTER VI.

BY STRAMMER TARN.

It was the middle of October. The September harvest had been reaped and carried; the sickles were laid aside for another year, and the barns were full to overflowing; it was getting late in the season for any stranger to be lingering among the hills, but still Captain Stondon remained on at the Farm contentedly. Had there been no outside world at all,—had there been no Norfolk estates, no London clubs, no Paris, no Vienna,— he could not have seemed better satisfied to stay, more loth to stir than was the case.

Each week, it is true, he said he must soon be journeying southward; but then each fresh week found him still loitering across the valley to the Parsonage; still contemplating the effects of the autumnal tints on heather, grass, and tree; still watching the changing leaves on the branches that overhung the waterfall; still climbing the mountain sides, or wending his way to Strammer Tarn.

His arm had knit by this time, and although he continued to carry a stick, his ankle was almost strong again. He had drunk in a new draught amid the hills; he had gone back years, seated by the ingle nook, wandering among the heather; he had forgotten the weary years of his lonely manhood; and he was taking his youth—his unenjoyed, unprofitable youth—once more in the autumn of existence, and living it out again, thoroughly, happily, among the mountains of Cumberland.

He had found rest; he had found contentment. He had put the gloom of the shadow that formerly rested over his soul aside, and in that strange household, surrounded by young people, by nature, by activity, by life, and hope, and strength, he grew light-hearted, and with boys became as a boy, capable of enjoying each day that dawned upon the earth.

To be sure, at first he found it no easy matter either to understand what the lads said, or to make them comprehend exactly what he said in return. They had run so wild about the hills; they had mixed so much with the boys in the valley; they had grown up so entirely amid Cumberland sounds and Cumberland associations, that their every sentence contained some word which seemed strange and unaccustomed in the ear of their guest.

But, as a rule, Phemie was close at hand to comprehend and to explain. She it was who told him what Duncan meant by a " bainer " way to Strammer Tarn; by a "whang" of bread; by Mrs. Aggland being in a "taaking," and by calling Davy a " tyke."

With her lovely face turned up to his she would laugh out at his perplexities, and then make darkness clear before him. She would scold Duncan in a pretty womanly way for using the Cumberland dialect, and then " draw him out " for the officer's benefit. She would dance over the moors and the heather, as Duncan sometimes told her,

like a " rannigal," and then she would sit down
quietly at the edge of the Black Tarn, and talk to
Captain Stondon about her childhood, while she
pulled off her bonnet and wreathed the broom
and the wild flowers into garlands for her hair.

It was not an exciting life, but it was peaceful,
without being solitary. Since his boyhood, since
the time which lay almost half a century behind
him, Captain Stondon had never known what it
was to enter any house, not even his own, and to
feel he was crossing the threshold of home. To
rest and be thankful ; to live and rejoice ; to look
on the merest excursion as a pleasure ; to understand that leisure was never given to man solely
that he might employ his leisure in killing time,
—these things were to Captain Stondon almost
like revelations, and he accepted the new light
and lay down and basked in its glory joyfully.

Home ! What makes a home, I wonder ?
Looking back in the after days to that queer
old Cumberland farm-house across the sea, thinking of its quiet, and its happiness, even whilst
surrounded by the warmth, and the beauty, and

the gaiety of southern climes, Captain Stondon came to believe that home is not so much one great fact, as the total of an aggregation of trifles; that the way the sunbeams steal into the windows, the particular description of rose that is trained round the casements, the scent of the honeysuckle which climbs over the porch, the plan of the house, the position of the doors, the placing of the furniture, the eccentricities of the servants, the tricks of the animals,—all these odds and ends frame and fit together so as to make one great and perfect whole, which shall remain stamped on the memory when the soul has sickened of lordly mansions, and the brain refuses to remember the cold bare discomfort of houses that are not homes, that lack the thousand-and-one charms which often-times form a chain strong enough to bind the heart of some great man to the lowliest cottage standing by the wayside of life. It is the sunlight on the floor, it is the trees that overshadow the roof, it is the springing of the turf under foot, it is the per-fume of the flowers stealing in through the open windows, it is the grouping of a circle round a blazing fire, it is the tone of the voices, it is a series of sensations which engross the soul, and forge fetters around the wisest and the best.

The Hill Farm had every element of home strong about it. The sunbeams seemed never weary of shining on it, as if they loved the very stones in its walls; the roses put out buds and bloomed even in the frost. There was no such piece of grass in any nobleman's park as Mr. Aggland boasted beneath his parlour windows. Most part of the year the little garden was a blaze of flowers, but specially in the autumn the place seemed on fire with scarlet verbenas and Tom Thumb geraniums, with nasturtiums, and stately dahlias, and heliotropes, and fuchsias.

The poor man's flowers, when he takes care of them, always bloom before the buds burst in the parterre of his richer neighbour. As though God loved best him to whom He gives the least, He seems to send His sun and His rain with richer blessing to the one than to the other, and the little crop comes up more abundantly before the

door of the cottager than the great crop is ever
seen to do in the broad fields that are owned by
his landlord and master the squire. It was thus
at any rate with the Agglands—what they planted,
they gathered; what they watered and tended,
grew up to perfection. The great man of Grassenfel, Lord Wanthorpe, who kept six gardeners,
could not for wages obtain such efficient help as
Mr. Aggland brought round him after school-hours
every afternoon.

Delving and digging, watering and wheeling,
clearing and weeding, was fun to the lads—exercise to their father. With all his quotations, he
did not bring them up in idleness: not one of the
boys but could clean a horse, harness and drive
him, saddle and ride him, as well as any groom in
the country.

They could have bought and sold, those lads;
you might have sent them to market, and trusted
their judgment of a drove of beasts as well as that
of any bailiff. They would argue—Duncan more
particularly—with their father, knotty points of
colour, vein, and shape; they would stand with

their hands in their pockets, and criticise a two-
year-old as gravely as any *habitué* of Tattersall's.
They were great on sheep; they were learned
about dogs; occasionally they were pleased to drop
some words of wisdom about hens and chickens for
the edification of Captain Stondon; and concerning geese and turkeys they were a vast deal better
informed than the person who took charge of
those interesting animals in the poultry yard at
Marshlands.

Altogether, brought up in the country, the boys
were *au fait* in matters appertaining to the
country. They knew all about soils; they spoke
lovingly of manures. In advance of their farming
brethren in the matter of rotation crops, they were
apt, following their father's lead, to be a little
dogmatical and wearisome on the subject of ex-
hausting and recruiting the ground.

Mr. Aggland piqued himself on having brought
the "best ideas of all nations" into practical use
on his little farm; and the days came when,
knowing more about the man, about the difficulties he had surmounted, the troubles he had

struggled through, Captain Stondon acknowledged that, possibly, no other individual could have made as much of the Hill Farm as Mr. Aggland ; that he had kept a large family well, and brought them up respectably, where a different father might have found it a hard struggle to provide such a tribe of children with dry bread off so bare and inhospitable a corner of the earth.

The Hill Farm was cheap, the Hill Farm was picturesque, but it was likewise poor and inaccessible.

" No man before me was ever able to pay his rent out of the ground," said Mr. Aggland, with excusable vanity; " each successive tenant planted on the hill, as he would have planted in the valley, and the result was disappointment and ruin. I, who had never been a farmer, was looked upon as a madman for supposing I should succeed where practical men had failed ; but, remembering Seneca's axiom, that 'Science is but one,' I laboured on with patience and in hope. And through all my labour I had pleasure. I have been happier here than I was in the days when

my prospects were brighter. Did you ever read
Burns' 'Twa Dogs,' sir?"

If Captain Stondon had thought saying " Yes "
would have saved him the quotation, he might
have replied falsely; but, knowing that the verse
was sure to come in any case, he answered " No."

"The poem is neither more nor less than a
comparison between riches and poverty," explained Mr. Aggland. " It is a conversation between two dogs; between one whose

> " '—Locked, lettered, brass, braw collar,
>   Showed him the gentleman and scholar,'

and another—

> " 'A ploughman's collie . . . a gude and faithfu' tyke.'

The gentleman—' Cæsar '—is made to say—

> " ' I see how folk live that hae riches,
>   But surely poor folk maun be wretches.'

Was not it, sir, a clever notion putting in the
mouth of a dog the thought that passes so often
through the heart of a man?"

"And what does the other answer?" asked
Captain Stondon.

"He says with truth that 'they are nae sae

wretched 's ane wad think,' and then goes on to what I was going to remark at first,—

> " ' An' tho' fatigued wi' close employment,
> A blink o' rest 's a sweet enjoyment.'

That was it, sir. After I had done my day's work I could enjoy rest as I had never enjoyed anything in the time when I was idle and earning my bread easily, and, as I think now, meanly. And even now I feel it a pleasure to see the seed I have helped to sow springing up, and bearing fruit in the Lord's due season. Although toil has been my lot, I can sing, with the sweetest of our modern poets,

> " ' There is not a creature, from England's king
> To the peasant that delves the soil,
> That knows half the pleasure the seasons bring,
> If he have not his share of toil.'

Look at the farm, sir. It was like moorland when I came here first, and now I pay my rent and keep my family off it, and I have a trifle besides in the Grassenfel Bank. To be sure, if I were to die, things might go hard with the wife and children, but there are few in any station who can do more than support their boys and girls, and

give them education. Duncan certainly might
soon take the farm, and Phemie would help him.
It may be that some day they will make a match,
and then——"

"The man is come over from Grassenfel about
the sheep, uncle," interrupted Phemie at this
juncture; and as Mr. Aggland left Captain Stondon to attend to business, the officer turned and
looked strangely at the girl whose probable future
he had just heard sketched out.

There was a colour in her face which seemed to
imply that she had heard likewise; but, half-an-
hour afterwards, when she and all her cousins,
Duncan included, accompanied their guest up the
hill and over the heather to Strammer Tarn, her
step was as light and her laugh rang out as clear
as though there were no such thing as marrying
or giving in marriage on earth.

"A nice fate truly," thought Captain Stondon,
savagely; " to keep a girl like that making butter
and darning stockings all her life. Such hair,
such features, such a complexion, such grace
wasted on a raw-boned Cumberland lout. Great

Heavens ! such sacrilege should not be permitted in a Christian country. What would she like, I wonder. It might be worth while trying to get to know what she thinks on the subject."

But, frank as she seemed, what she hoped, what she feared, what she dreamed, were things Phemie Keller was never going to tell to Captain Stondon. In the world she had but one confidante; the hard-featured, high-cheeked, loud-voice Scotchwoman, who had been with her from her childhood, who had come with her from Scotland, who had served the first Mrs. Aggland, and was now serving the second, and who loved blue-eyed, bright-haired, laughing, light-hearted Phemie Keller with a love passing the love of woman.

Sitting on the boulders that lay near the edge of the Strammer Tarn, with her cousin Helen's head resting on her lap, with the clear October sky above, with the black rocks frowning on her girlish beauty, with the dark water at her feet, Phemie talked to the stranger of everything save the dreams she dreamed when she lay wide awake in her little bed at night, save the romantic future

she and Peggy sketched out when "croonin'" together over the winter fire in the kitchen, or
basking in the glorious sunlight of some summer
Sunday afternoon.

Did he think the girl unconscious of her loveliness?—did he imagine that, though she might seem
merely "pretty" to her neighbours, Phemie Keller
did not know she was the making of as beautiful
a woman as ever turned men's heads and caused
honest hearts to ache for love of her? Is not
beauty a talent, and did not she know God had
given her that one talent, at any rate? He had
lived long, and he had seen much, but he fell into
error here. Phemie was fully aware of the extent
of her own charms. All her earlier years she had
been "my bonnie, bonnie bairn" to somebody;
and now her glass, small though it might be, told
the little lady she was beautiful, whilst, if other
proof were wanting, Mr. Conbyr's entreaties that
she would set her face against vanity, and the
whispered compliments of young Mr. Fagg, the
surgeon, from Grassenfel, should have fully convinced her of the fact.

And so while they talked together, and while Captain Stondon thought he was reading this girl's nature as though it were an easy book Phemie was keeping back the dreams and the visions that made her young life tolerable to her. She could sit contentedly at work because airy castles rose to the sky at her lightest bidding; she could go about the housework cheerily, thinking of the future day which was to dawn and free her from all drudgery and all toil, and she could talk frankly and naturally to this middle-aged man, who tried to draw her out because he was as far from her ideal of a lover, or a husband, or a hero as Mr. Fagg, or even her hard-headed cousin Duncan himself.

"My father was an officer too," Phemie was pleased to explain on the afternoon in question; "but he was only a lieutenant,—Lieutenant Keller; I have got his portrait at the farm, if you would like to see it. He looks so young and so handsome," the girl added, with a tremor in her voice, and she bent her head over her favourite Helen, touching the child's dark locks lovingly as she spoke.

"You resemble him then, doubtless," suggested Captain Stondon, gallantly.

"I believe I do," she said, apparently without noticing the implied compliment; "but my mother was fair too. I remember her with such a colour in her face that, if people had not known to the contrary, they would have said she was painted. She died when she was only one-and-twenty; but I remember her. Uncle tells me they were both little more than boy and girl—boy and girl," Phemie repeated, with her eyes straining over the Black Tarn, as though she saw the shadowy forms of those dead parents standing on the opposite shore.

Up to that moment Captain Stondon had taken Mr. Conbyr's statement for granted; but now he began to waver in his faith. If she were really illegitimate, Phemie's uncle would never have spoken to her about her parents so unreservedly; she would never have been suffered to retain the portrait of which she had just made mention.

Hitherto the question of her birth had been one studiously avoided by the officer; but suddenly he became desirous to know all about Miss

Keller's parents, and began to insinuate questions accordingly.

"Was her father dead or abroad?" he ventured, after a pause.

"Oh, he died before my mother," Phemie answered; "and she never held up her head after, Peggy says. It was at Malta we were then, and my mother brought his body back to his own people, and then returned to her father's house with me."

"Why did she not remain with her husband's family?" asked Captain Stondon.

"Because they would not have her remain, and because she thought a Scotch Duncan as good as an English Keller any day, and would not be looked down on by them. The Kellers are great folks somewhere, or think themselves great folks; and they never forgave my father for marrying a poor minister's daughter. He told her to go to them after his death for my sake, and she went because he bade her; but they turned her from the door, and—and——"

Phemie bowed her head and sobbed aloud as she tried to finish her sentence. She had heard her mother's wrongs so often spoken of,—she had heard Peggy M'Nab tell so pathetically how that young creature, repulsed by her husband's kindred, had travelled home to the old manse to die, that she could not speak without weeping as she recalled the story.

Home to die! home to the familiar places she had left so few years before to look her last on them ere she passed from earth for ever;—home to the lonely manse by the desolate sea-shore;— home to the well-remembered rooms where she could lie and listen to the long roll of the Atlantic waves as they came booming up against the rocky coast;—home to the haunts and the friends of her girlhood;—home—or, as Peggy said so plaintively—

" Hame, hame, puir thing, to dee."

Phemie could not talk of it calmly; Phemie could scarcely talk of the manse itself calmly, let alone of her mother; and whilst Captain Stondon retraced his steps towards Tordale in the gathering twilight, with Duncan and Helen and Phemie beside him, and the other children running on towards home as fast as their little legs could carry them, he made up his mind to have some talk with Mr. Aggland, and discover how he might best advance that eccentric individual's views, and do something at the same time for Phemie Keller.

CHAPTER VII.

THE AGGLAND INTERIOR.

THE short October day was drawing to a close when the party reached home ; and it had grown so dark by the time they reached the Hill Farm, that candles were lighted and curtains drawn, and the tea-things set, awaiting their arrival. Amazingly cozy looked the parlour, with sofa pulled round beside the fire, a steaming kettle on the hob, and coals piled high blazing up the chimney.

Though the furniture was of the plainest, the room seemed homelike and cheerful to Captain Stondon, who was greeted by Mr. Aggland with—

"You must have found Strammer Tarn unusually attractive this afternoon. Were you watching 'Autumn like a faint old man sit down—by the wayside a-weary?' Have you brought an appetite back with you from the hills? Mr. Conbyr has been here begging that you will dine with him to-morrow. So, in common courtesy, you are in for two sermons—two of *his* sermons—good lack! Nevertheless 'tis a good man 'Gray, with his eyes uplifted to Heaven.' I do think Mr. Conbyr does try to keep both eyes and soul uplifted; for which reason I make the children write down his sermons as well as they can after they come from church. In a literary point of view, what he says may not be super-excellent, but the words of a good man must always hold something worth remembering. Now, Phemie, let us have some tea," finished Mr. Aggland, with the air of a person who felt that, having delivered himself of a Christian sentiment, he deserved some refreshment after it.

Dutifully obedient, the girl poured out the tea, and when he had handed a cup to his wife, who sat knitting by the fire, and another to Captain Stondon, who was contemplating Phemie, Mr. Aggland duly and solemnly stirred up the sugar from the bottom, and then tasted the infusion.

"Wormwood! wormwood!" he exclaimed, surveying the tea with astonishment and Phemie with reproach. "There's rue for you," he added, turning to Captain Stondon, "and here's some for me. We may call it herb of grace o' Sundays, but it is quite a different matter to drink it any evening in the week. What the deuce, child, have you done to it? Salts and senna—soda and bark! ugh!" and Mr. Aggland began putting all the cups back on the tray.

"I will keep mine," said Mrs. Aggland defiantly. "If yours does not please you, have some more made. As Phemie was out wasting her time as usual on the hills, I wet the tea; but I won't wet it again—what I brew never contents you."

Having concluded this pleasant sentence, Mrs. Aggland resumed her knitting, while Mr. Aggland, having muttered something that sounded very like "Damn the tea!" directed his conversation towards his guest, who had long doubted the prudence of the farmer's second choice, and who felt more and more convinced of the fact of its imprudence every day he passed in the house.

Not a virago was Mrs. Aggland; not a noisy,

headstrong, passionate woman. There was no quarrelling and making up with her. She did not fly into a passion one moment, and calm down the next. She simply "nagged." There is no other word that I know of to express her mode of proceeding, or I would use it.

Man could not delight her, nor woman neither, if the man and the woman chanced to be of her own household. From the time she rose in the morning till she laid her pinched, discontented face on the pillow at night, the thing was never done, by child or adult, that pleased her; and the person who seemed able to displease her most was Phemie Keller.

In her youth, which takes us back to a somewhat remote period, Mrs. Aggland had been reckoned rather a beauty by the young men in her own class of life. She was a belle of the genteel sentimental style; laced tight, minced her words, drank vinegar to keep herself pale, wore her ugly drab hair in curls, held her head on one side, simpered like a fool when spoken to, and was altogether a superior young person, who married, in her two-and-thirtieth year, Mr. King, a struggling grocer in Lancaster.

Mr. King survived the unhappy event for five years, at the end of which time he died, leaving her a small business and four children. When or how Mr. Aggland first became acquainted with the widow, he never informed his neighbours. All any one could say for certain was, that he took her to wife, and that she brought him some money and the children aforesaid. So much the world knew; but Mr. Aggland knew, besides, that he had made a bad bargain, an irreparable blunder, that life had been a harder struggle with him than ever during the six years which had elapsed since his second marriage.

There were already three young pledges of affection—two aged five years, and a burly child just able to run about alone—born to him of this ill-assorted union.

What the future held, it might be difficult for him to say, but if it held many more children, Mr. Aggland confessed to his own heart that the prospect was not inviting. Had it not been for

Phemie, he scarcely knew how the house would have gone on at all; and Mrs. Aggland hated Phemie for reasons which I am about to tell.

Mrs. Aggland had been a beauty relatively, Phemie was a beauty positively. Mrs. Aggland had taken pains to make and keep herself "genteel." Without any arts or devices Phemie looked a lady even in her aunt's cast-off finery.

Mrs. Aggland had been given to melody in her younger days. Her rendering of pathetic songs, such as, "Oh! no, we never mention her," "The Soldier's Tear," "The Banks of Allan Water," and others of the same stamp, had won for her immense applause from her numerous admirers. The high note in the "Banks of Allan Water," and the *rallentando* passage in the "Soldier's Tear," when very softly and with the help of quavers and semi-quavers the tear is wiped away, used always to produce a sensation, and it was therefore no wonder that Mrs. Aggland resented Phemie's voice as a personal injury, and detested her for possessing it.

Even the children liked best to hear their

cousin sing. They would leave the "Lass of Gowrie" for "Love's Ritornella," and "Young Lochinvar" for "Allan-a-dale." It is not given to every *prima donna* to make way for a younger comer gracefully, and Mrs. Aggland was only human ; for which reason, it may be, she would not have repined against the decrees of Providence if Phemie had caught bronchitis and lost her voice.

Further, though Mrs. Aggland had brought her husband some small dowry, she had brought him incumbrances likewise ; and this girl—this Hagar in the household—this Mordecai at the gate— possessed her trifling portion too, a hundred pounds, the principal and interest and com- pound interest of which were to be hers on coming of age, or on marriage.

Mr. Aggland could have used the money had he liked—taken it in payment for her board and lodging; but he had settled that not even in their blackest distress was the girl's "tocher" to be touched, and the money was kept intact ac- cordingly.

Heaven help us! perhaps the man had more than hoped she and Duncan would spend it together, and try and stock a small homestead for themselves, where he could visit them, and smoke and quote and sing in peace.

Had he any other dream? Did he think that Duncan, with his turn for mechanics, with that passion for making a pump and a steam-engine which seems to be the besetting sin of English lads—the snare and the delusion that Satan in these latter days has devised for the disappointment and confusion of parents—with his dogged perseverance, and his intensely Scotch hard-headedness, might rise to eminence in the future? Perhaps that was the reason why he kept the boy at school long after the age when most farmers' sons had completed their education and relapsed into boorishness for ever.

Mr. Aggland was so fond of talking about Watt, Arkwright, Strutt, Foley, Petty, and a number of other self-made men, as to suggest the idea that far away down in his heart he was nourishing ambitious hopes concerning his eldest son's worldly advancement. One thing, however, was certain. He wanted Phemie and Duncan to grow up into lovers and to marry in due time, for which reason he encouraged the visits of none of the young men who would perhaps have thought themselves good enough to aspire to the hand of Miss Keller ; and consequently Miss Keller had heard as few compliments and blushed as little at pretty rustic speeches as the strictest matron could have desired.

Nevertheless Phemie knew she was pretty, and so did Mrs. Aggland, which mutual knowledge by no means conduced to the maintenance of peace and quietness between the pair.

Moreover, Phemie was far more clever than Mrs. Aggland ; more clever and quick not merely at catching up book learning, but at needlework, at household duties, and in all other practical affairs. Given opportunity, there could be no doubt but that the girl would have been as accomplished and well-informed as she was pretty. Even as matters stood, she had got a curious smattering of knowledge into her head. She had

read and re-read all the books in her uncle's
singularly miscellaneous library. He had taught
her what he knew of French; she had learned to
play the guitar almost without his help; and Mrs.
Aggland, looking askance, prophesied that such
" goings on," " such ways," " such notions," would
bring Phemie to ruin; while there were not a few
in the neighbourhood—Mr. Conbyr himself, worthy
man, amongst the number—who sympathised with
Mrs. Aggland, and thought Phemie was being
fairly spoiled by her eccentric and imprudent
uncle.

"Even to the making of the tea," muttered
Mrs. Aggland, as she went on with her knitting,
and with one light-coloured eye watched Phemie
pouring out the fresh infusion, " I might as well
be nobody. He had better never have married at
all."

Which was undeniably true; at any rate, he
had better never have married at all than married
her, and he was perhaps thinking something of
the kind even while he went on talking to Captain
Stondon about indifferent subjects.

All at once Mrs. Aggland broke into the conversation. She did not like being left on one side so completely. Even the pleasure of indulging her bad temper, and seeing other people uncomfortable, was dearly purchased at the price of such neglect; therefore, when Captain Stondon was making some remarks about the loneliness and desolation of Strammer Tarn, she laid down her knitting, a sure sign of truce, and observed that she had not seen Strammer Tarn. "I have never been to Grassenfel since I came home to this house," she said; "except to church once in a way, and to a chance prayer-meeting at a neighbour's, I never set foot across the threshold."

"You find so many home occupations, doubtless," suggested Captain Stondon.

"Yes, and it is the children," she replied. "Where there is so much work to be done, and so few to do it, where there are so many mouths to fill, and so much planning needed to fill them, it stands to sense I can't be running over the hills like a girl. I can't leave things to go to wrack and ruin by themselves."

" I am certain," said Captain Stondon, gallantly, " that nothing can go to ruin in the same house with you."

" I am sure it is very good of you to think so. It is not every one that would say as much, though I do work early and late, though I can say with a safe conscience I never eat the bread of idleness," remarked Mrs. Aggland, darting a look towards her husband, who coolly said :—

" If you mean me, Prissy, my dear, you are quite mistaken. I am willing to say all Captain Stondon said, and more ; I am willing to say all you said, and more. You rise early, you take your rest late, you do not eat the bread of idleness, you eat that of carefulness—what more ? ' The man in the world who shall report he has a better wife, let him in nought be trusted.' "

"Capital, Mr. Aggland! a most happy quotation," remarked Captain Stondon. For Phemie's sake ; for Phemie, who was now out of the room putting the younger children to bed, he wanted to throw oil on the waters, to calm the tempest that had literally arisen in a teapot.

" Many a one wondered," went on Mrs. Aggland, " how I ever could think of marrying again after losing the kind, good, blessed husband, for which I were a-wearing weeds when I met with Mr. A. And, most of all, how I ever came to marry a man with children. I had made up my mind never to leave off widow's caps no more. I had set down my foot against matrimony and every folly of the sort, when Mr. Aggland came and persuaded me to change my mind. To hear him talk now some-times, nobody would think he had tried so hard to get me, for I had a'most sworn never to put a step-father over my boys; but you see, sir, what it is to be tempted," and Mrs. Aggland executed an idiotic giggle, while Captain Stondon an-swered :—

"See, rather, madam, what it is to be tempting." Which speech put the *ci-devant* beauty into a seventh heaven of good temper, and straightway the pair began a little skirmish of assertion and retort.

" He, the captain, was only making fun of an old woman like herself."

" No, upon his honour, he had merely stated a self-evident fact."

" Ten years before she might have been, at least some folks had said so; but now, with a growing-up family about her——"

" She failed to rate herself as highly as her friends did," put in Captain Stondon.

" The care of children soon put all those kind of foolish notions out of a woman's head; not that even in her youngest days she had been given to vanities, and now she was a mother——

" Ah, Captain Stondon," she finished pathetically, " *you* don't know what it is to be a mother——"

" And he doesn't want to know, I am sure," interrupted Mr. Aggland; which statement was so incontrovertibly true, that the officer could not for the life of him help laughing at his host's way of putting things.

Just then Phemie re-entered the room, carrying a bonnet in one hand and her workbox in the other. Having her little vanities too, she had asked a neighbour to bring her some ribbon from

Grassenfel, and her heart was set on trimming her bonnet that very Saturday night with the laudable view of wearing it the next morning in church.

There was no absolute sinfulness, we will conclude, in this desire; but Mrs. Aggland fired up on the spot to denounce such wickedness.

"Was it not enough that she had wasted her whole afternoon? was she going to waste the evening as well? With a hole in Duncan's jacket; with the pockets in her uncle's coat like sieves; with Helen's plaid dress wanting lining; with all the children needing stockings mended for the morrow, was she going to sit down and make up finery for herself? She, Mrs. Aggland, wondered how Phemie could have the face to go to church after such selfishness. She wanted to know what her Maker would think of her when He saw her sitting there with new trimmings on her bonnet, and the children's toes, poor dears, coming through their socks."

"Phemie mended twenty pairs this morning,"

said Duncan, who had followed his cousin into the room ; " I counted them."

" Then she can get to Helen's frock," answered Mrs. Aggland.

" Now let's have an end of this," broke in Mr. Aggland, angrily. " I won't have the girl made a slave of by anybody. Go on with your bonnet, Phemie."

But the beauty had been taken off the ribbons for the girl. She could not see them for tears ; and so, putting all her little finery aside, she assured her uncle that she did not care, that her work could wait, that she had forgotten Helen's frock, and would rather do it.

As she spoke, with the tears just trembling in her voice, with her pretty hands putting the lace, and ribbons, and net hurriedly on one side, with her head bent down so that no one might see she was crying, Mr. Aggland suddenly caught Captain Stondon looking earnestly at her with an expression in his face which made the farmer's heart stand still.

The man loved her ! and if winter's snows had

covered the green wheat in May, Mr. Aggland could not have been more shocked or more surprised.

For this he was staying among the hills—for this he was putting up with such poor accommodation as the farm afforded—for this he was complimentary to Mrs. Aggland—for this he had a pleasant word for every man, woman, and child about the place.

For this——How could he have been so blind? how could he have been such a fool? What was Mrs. Aggland's scolding in comparison to such a discovery? As to sit and talk without making a fool of himself till he had leisure to think over the matter, it was not to be attempted.

"Perhaps your aunt will give you a holiday tonight, Phemie?" he said; "and let us have some music."

It was Mr. Aggland who spoke; but his voice sounded so strange and altered, that every one in the room turned and looked at him with involuntary surprise. Even his wife was astonished into saying that if Phemie had done the socks, the

other things could "let be;" while Captain Stondon, reading in his host's face something of what
was passing within, woke at the same moment to
a vague kind of comprehension that he had dug
up his heart from the dead woman's grave, that
he had swerved from the old allegiance at last,
and that he was as hopelessly in love with a pair
of bright eyes, with a glory of auburn hair, with
a young, young girl, as the most foolish lad of
nineteen.

Well! well! a man may catch a fever at any
age. There is no law in the Statute Book, as far
as I am aware, which forbids or prevents his
doing so.

Meantime Duncan fetched in his father's violin,
and Duncan's brother, Donald, together with
Helen Aggland and John and Prissy King, came
trooping into the room laden with music-books.
By degrees a younger Aggland and two more
Kings straggled out of the kitchen into the parlour, and if the other children had not been satis-
factorily tucked up in bed, they would have
toddled down stairs also to hear "the singing."

When a man's natural language chances to be music, like Mr. Aggland's, the household generally is apt to hear a little more melody than proves agreeable. At the Hill Farm, however, everybody's language seemed to be music. Peggy crooned Scotch ballads all day long in the kitchen ; Mrs. Aggland's shrill treble was to be heard uplifted in " The Maid of Llangollen," " He was a Knight of low degree," and other songs of the same style and period. Duncan for everlasting was shouting out, " Sing, sing, sing—who sings ? " which performance he occasionally varied with " The Pilgrim Fathers," while the lesser fry chirped out snatches of old airs, mixing up hymns and Jacobite tunes in the strangest way imaginable. Mr. Aggland himself generally went through his daily duties to the tune of " The Hundredth Psalm," and swore at his refractory labourers between the bars.

"All people that on earth " was, accordingly, what he selected to lead off with when he had screwed up his violin, and his wife kindly took the treble, which would perhaps have sounded all the

better had she not occasionally interrupted her
performance to box some of the children's ears, to
" drat their noise," and to wonder if any woman
ever was so plagued as she. With the tears wiped
off her cheeks, with her lovely eyes bright as ever,
Phemie, stitching away at Helen's frock, sometimes interposed a sweet second, sometimes, when
her sense of the ludicrous was touched, looked
mischievously across at Captain Stondon, and made
him smile and turn away his head in spite of
himself.

" What the devil are you about, Prissy ! " was
one of Mr. Aggland's most usual sentences in the
middle of a hymn ; and when every now and then
he hit Duncan a rap over the head for singing a
false note, the punishment tested the officer's
gravity severely.

It would have been a curious scene that for
any stranger to look in on. By the fire sat Mrs.
Aggland, with her cap a little awry, with the cor-
ners of her eyes drawn down, with her mouth wide
open, with her head on one side. Excepting Mr.
Aggland, no one, I think, ever pulled such absurdly

ugly faces while singing as the mistress of the Hill Farm; but the master eclipsed her; every hair on his head quivered as he sang; not a muscle remained still as he shook, and quavered, and indulged in extempore roulades. The way he swung himself about, the manenr in which he swayed from side to side, the perfect desperation with which he sang, the earnestness with which he cursed,—these things all tended to make Phemie misbehave herself, all conduced to fits of coughing, and to suspicious attention to Helen's frock.

"Ech, Lord save us!" Peggy was ejaculating in the kitchen; "Maister 'ull burst his pipes, surely. He ought to bring roun' the forty-foot ladder if he wants to get up to that. My certy, he is at it again!" And Peggy absolutely paused in her work to listen.

A little back from the fire sat Captain Stondon, with a batch of the children round him, thinking of the long ago past, of the pleasant, yet fleeting, present. For his years he was a young-looking man; he carried his fifty-five summers lightly, and stooped no more under them than if fifteen had been subtracted from their number. India had not aged him. There was still about him something of the same dash and *bonhommie* which had won friends and gained love for the young lieutenant of, say, thirty years before. His brown hair was as yet unmixed with grey, his light-blue eyes had not lost their keenness of vision, their honesty of expression. If there was nothing romantic about his appearance, there was something which yet made any one with whom he came in contact feel instinctively that he was true ; if he was not handsome, he was not plain. He looked like what he was, an English squire, of good birth, in easy circumstances, strong, hearty, middle-aged. He had grown younger since he came to the Hill Farm. Perhaps the children climbing up his knees, perhaps the total rest, perhaps the long idle days spent in watching Davy stand on his hind legs smoking ; in seeing Duncan getting bare-back on unbroken colts, and gallop them round the fields ; in laughing at the tosses the younger fry got while riding a favourite ram and an ill-conditioned calf up and down the paddock ;

and in wandering over the hills to Strammer Tarn, had contributed to this result : but in any case the fact was undeniable, Captain Stondon had retrograded in years ; and if all went on well, he bade fair to retrograde a few more. He would have liked the singing to continue for ever, so that he might look at Phemie's white hands, and snowy neck, and pretty face, without let or hindrance. But all earthly things must come to an end ; and after Mr. Aggland had indulged the company with the serenade from "Don Pasquale" solo, and the assembled congregation had sung the "Evening Hymn," in no one line of which Phemie could join, for fear of laughing out loud at her uncle, the concert would have concluded, but for this.

"Johnny," whispered Captain Stondon to one of the young Kings while the "Evening Hymn" was still in progress, "get your cousin to sing something alone to the guitar, and I will send you down the strongest knife I can find in London— one with four blades. Ask her yourself, you know."

Whereupon the young imp struck his closed mouth with his hand, and the moment Mr. Aggland put aside the violin, began tormenting Phemie for one song—only one—only—only—only——

Which request Captain Stondon seconded, of course, and Duncan then joined in, telling their guest he should hear Phemie singing " Alice Gray."

" You just ought;" he added, a sentence that of course raised the officer's curiosity to fever pitch.

" I may never hear it," he pleaded, " if you do not sing it to-night, for I shall probably have to leave early in the week;" and thus urged, Phemie, blushing a good deal, took the guitar, and after tuning it began—

> " She's all my fancy painted her,
>   She's lovely, she's divine ;
> But her heart it is another's,
>   And it never can be mine.
> Yet loved I as man never loved,
>   A love without decay—
> Oh ! my heart, my heart is breaking
>   For the love of Alice Gray."

I dare say there are few who read these pages that know anything of the old ballads which were sung by the grandmothers of the present generation. New words and new music have succeeded

to the simple airs and the homely verses that yet
had strength enough in them to make many a
man's heart throb faster as he heard ; and it is very
rarely—once in a dozen years or so—that any one
strikes the well-remembered chords and wakes
the old harmony once more.   Half a lifetime had
gone over Captain Stondon's head since the ballad
Phemie Keller sung had sounded in his ears before ; but the years seemed to fade away from
his memory as he listened, and he was young
again, sitting back in a crowded drawing-room,
that he might hide the tears he could not help
shedding.   Ah me ! ah me ! that men's hearts
should keep so young, whilst their bodies grow so
old—that the pains of youth should stay with us
when the hopeful buoyancy of youth is gone—
that a touch should make the blood flow out fast
as ever, when there is no sap left behind to enable
the bare tree to put forth green leaves and bright
buds of promise—that tears should well up into
the eyes when the capacity for smiling has left
the lips—that we should live through all the fever
and trouble, and fret and worry, we thought left

so far behind, at the tone of a voice, at the sound of an air.

The man's heart had not broken then; was it to be broken now?

Had he kept the toy, defaced and battered though it might be, all these years, to the end that a girl should destroy it at last? Was it only the olden memories that made him pause for a moment ere he thanked Phemie for her song? Was it not rather that a new Alice Gray had crossed his path, more fair, more divine, than the Alice Gray of old? A young, fresh, ingenuous Alice, with the truest eyes, the most exquisite hair, the most heavenly voice, man had ever conceived of? If he should love this Alice, would his heart not break? With nothing before, with everything behind him, what would the hereafter of his life prove, if he had to leave that sweet face amid the Cumberland hills while he went back again into the dreary, lonely world, solitary and objectless. He would win her love, he would make her love him. Surely his position, his wealth, his personal appearance, his manners, were far above anything

Miss Keller was likely to meet with at the Hill Farm. He would be so good to her and hers; he would be so tender with her, so thoughtful, that for very gratitude she must learn to love him. He would take her away, he would show her foreign countries, he would surround her with every luxury. She should walk "in silk attire." Rich and rare should be the gems wherewith he would deck her; life to her should be as a fairy tale; money and lands would be of value to° him at last; everything he possessed—name, station, wealth— should be put to a use for her—for this Cinderella, whom he meant to convert into a princess, if it pleased her to let him do so. All the old tales, all the old ballads, came into his head the wrong way at the same moment, for alas! *he* was the rich suitor, and not the young penniless wooer; it was *he* who was thinking of offering the " rigs of land, the sheep and the kye, the gowd and the siller," which never ought to be owned by fortunate lovers. He was reading the poems of all times with an inverted meaning, and he might have gone to bed that night happy, and dreamed the sweet dreams of the long and long ago but for Mr. Aggland.

"Phemie," said that gentleman, with a certain viciousness of manner, "since you have sung about one of the Grays for Duncan, will you sing about another for me? 'Auld Robin,' my dear."

What were the officer's thoughts after that, as he lay awake counting the weary hours that seemed to him to be walking slowly and lingeringly, like living things, backwards and forwards, over the eternal hills?

My reader, I scarcely know; but one thing is certain, that they were only a degree more bitter than those indulged in by Phemie's uncle, who, with eyes wide open, watched through the darkness his air castle vanishing away.

CHAPTER VIII.

ALL THE DIFFERENCE..

"You are right," said Mr. Aggland. " Home-keeping youth have ever homely wits ;" but the sentence did not flow glibly off his tongue, and the farmer stood for a moment after he had answered Captain Stondon, looking with his outward eyes it is true down the fair valley of Tordale, but trying with his mental vision to penetrate into the future which had suddenly become so misty and uncertain.

It was early in the week following that Saturday night when knowledge had come to two at least of the party at the Hill Farm. Captain Stondon was going to spend a few days at the Rectory before turning his back on Cumberland, and ere leaving the man who had been his friend in such sore need, he was trying to show his gratitude for the past, and to secure Mr. Aggland's services in the future—a double purpose which fettered his speech a little, and placed at once a certain embarrassment between himself and his host.

He was pleading to be allowed to do something for Duncan ; to be permitted to hold out a helping hand at this the turning point of his whole life.

" He has abilities," remarked Captain Stondon. " Why should he not have an opportunity of turning them to account ? He has brains ; why keep him here, where he will never have a chance of making a fortune out of them ? Let the boy go away and see the world. He will learn more in six months outside these mountains than he could learn in as many years under their shadow."

And in reply Mr. Aggland remarked, as already stated : " You are right. Home-keeping youth have ever homely wits. And yet——" he proceeded after a moment's pause, " judging from my own experience, I think it better for people who must content themselves with an humble sphere, never to be lifted above it. It is happier to be independent than rich; it is a fine thing to rise in the world, but it is a cursed thing to be patronised. My opinion is, that a man worth calling a man, ought to be able to say he owes all he owns, all he has enjoyed, to no other man living,—only to God and himself."

"But God makes men his instruments," suggested Captain Stondon.

"He may; but I doubt it," replied Mr. Aggland; "at least, I think we have no right to say the instruments we deliberately choose for ourselves were put in our way by the Almighty. Look at me. Should not I have been a happier man had no one ever said to me, 'Come out of your station, and be a gentleman, Aggland?' A gentleman, good lack, a gentleman?" and the farmer drew his hand up and down the sleeve of his threadbare coat, and looked at his patched shoes, at his coarse grey stockings, at his well-worn trousers, contemptuously as he spoke.

"Should you dislike telling me your story?" asked Captain Stondon, after a moment's hesitation. "Pardon me, if I seem impertinent; but your boy's case might be anything rather than analogous to your own."

"You are right again," was the reply, "since no two lives are ever precisely analogous, and yet each man who precedes us leaves his warning signal behind, showing where possible danger is lurking. Now, my life was cursed by patronage; and you offer patronage to my lad. You see my argument? My story, certainly. I will tell thee tales—

  " ' Of woful ages long ago betid :'

I will tell you the 'lamentable fall of me,' albeit it may be—

  " ' A tale told by an idiot,
   Signifying nothing.' "

"Let me be the judge of that," answered Captain Stondon, smiling in spite of himself; "let me hear your experience first, and then we can talk of Duncan's future afterwards."

"I must begin at the beginning, I suppose," said Mr. Aggland. "If you are not weary, shall we walk along the hill path while we talk? Where was I? oh, at my own birth, which happened on the sixth of April, eighteen hundred and one ; you can reckon that up, sir, hereafter, and find how old a man I am."

The blow was not intended, but Captain Stondon winced. He had made his *début* on this world's stage on the fourteenth of June, seventeen hundred and ninety, and it did not take him long to calculate how much older than Mr. Aggland that fact made him. Meantime the farmer proceeded :—

" I was not born of prosperous parents ; I was, on the contrary, born in 'poverty's low barren vale,' which is not nearly so desirable a vale to inhabit as poets usually imply. My father was a country schoolmaster, one who might have sat to Goldsmith for his picture. He loved children, he loved teaching, he loved learning ; but neither teaching, learning, nor children brought him much money. I can see him now," went on Mr. Aggland ; " see him sitting just where the sunbeams had cleared a space out for themselves in the middle of the dusty floor. The boys and girls are all quiet at their sums ; he is holding a slate, and explaining the Rule of Three to a child who stands beside him. That child was myself. I never knew him to be other than patient and gentle with me, for I was the youngest of a large family, the Benjamin of his age to him."

Mr. Aggland paused. For a moment the Cumberland hills faded from his eyes, and the old home, left so long before, yet remembered so distinctly, arose out of the years, and stood by the roadside, with the elder-tree shading it, with the duck-pond in front of it, with the half-acre of garden all a-glow with flowers surrounding it. He could see the sycamore under which he had lain whilst conning his Virgil and labouring through Ovid; and then the whole vision passed away, and he was looking at the reality of his life on a fine October morning, with Skillanscar and Helbeck towering to the sky, and the man whose life he had saved amongst those very rocks and crags walking beside him, waiting for him to proceed.

" He knew more than is usual with persons of his class," went on Mr. Aggland, " and he taught me to love learning as he did—to love it for its own sake, not for the sake of any money it might bring, of any advantage that might accrue from it. What he meant me to be, whether a schoolmaster like himself, or a clerk, or a labourer, I do not know, for at sixteen I had the misfortune to meet with a rich gentleman who took an interest in me. It happened in this way. My father had a brother living in a little seaport in Wales. He was a tailor, and pretty well to do, and he used to make us welcome to spend a week with him every summer, as the holidays came round. It was the last day of our stay, and I was hanging about the shore loth to leave the sea, for I loved it, when all at once there was a cry and a shout, and I saw a boy who had been bathing washed away by a wave and disappear. I guessed in a minute how it was; the lad had gone out beyond his depth, and could not swim. There were places where the sea deepened suddenly, and he had dropped on one of them. I did not know who he was, and if I had it would have made no difference; one life is as valuable as another I think now, and I suppose I thought the same then, if I thought at all. One boy is as good as another, whether he be the son of a king or the son of a peasant. I did not know who he was, and God is witness that, not knowing, I risked my life to save him willingly."

"And you did save him?" asked Captain Stondon.

"I ran a race with the sea for him," answered Mr. Aggland, a flush overspreading his hollow cheeks; "I fought for him, I got mad with the waves for trying to beat me out. Though it is thirty years since—thirty years within a trifle—I can remember, as if it was but yesterday, looking out over the waves seaward, and thinking I could follow him to Ireland, if need were, sooner than the waters should beat me. He went down twice. As he rose the third time I had him. I stretched my arm out over a wave and caught him. I could not have brought him back to land; but looking over the water, *not* towards Ireland this time, I saw help coming; and I kept him up till we were both pulled into the boat that had pushed off after me. I liked the sea up to that minute, sir ; I have hated it ever since. I could not put into words what I thought about it as I struggled to keep him and myself afloat till the boat came. I have never had a bad illness since, when that minute has not been reproduced for my benefit. I suppose it was fear came over me ; but I seemed to be in the power of some cruel enemy, with whom I could not reason, against whom I could not struggle ; I felt as if I was alone in the world out there—alone with the waters round and about me. I remember trying to hold on by the waves, and then after that there was a blank."

"Did they recover both of you ?" asked Captain Stondon.

"Yes—but they had hard work bringing the boy to life again. He was a small delicate lad, though two years older than myself; a motherless lad, an only son—the heir to a great property. His name was Worton ; and from the time he opened his eyes that day when I fought for him with the sea, till the hour when I closed the lids over them in Ischia, he never could bear me to leave him. And I never did leave him.

"Mr. Worton, who had seen the whole of the accident, was grateful, more grateful than there was any necessity for, and he offered to take me and bring me up with his own boy and provide for me, and allow my father a small annuity.

"If we had asked half his fortune, I think he would have given it to us, when he heard his son speak again. He need not have been so liberal as he was, and I have often wished since he had let us alone; but it seemed a fine thing to us then, and I went back with them to Worton Court as Master Reginald's friend—companion— what you will.

"We led an awfully idle life. All Mr. Worton's time was devoted to thinking what would best please his son; all Master Reginald's time was taken up trying to keep himself out of the grave. As Burns says, 'he met every face with a greeting like that of Balak to Balaam: "Come, curse me that East wind, and come, defy me the North."' It was such a labour to

him to live, that I have often wondered since
he did not wish to

> " ' Set up his everlasting rest.
> And shake the yoke of inauspicious stars
> From his world-wearied flesh.'

But he desired nothing of the kind. He enjoyed
existence as much as I have ever known any
one. He used to like lying on the sofa in the
winter time; lying on the grass in the summer.
He liked being read to, he liked to hear music;
he was fond of travelling by very slow stages,
in a very easy carriage; he enjoyed society, and
he loved me.

"We loved one another," went on Mr. Aggland,
after a pause. "'We were so mixed as meeting
streams, for he was I, I he.' The day came when
they tried to separate us, tried to make me
believe he would be better without me—tried to
make him believe I was no fit companion for
him; but we could not part till death took him,
and then I stood in the world alone. They had
made me what I was. Reginald had a tutor, but
we never learnt anything—never were expected

to learn. All my life had been for eight years spent in keeping him alive ; for eight years I did nothing but that ; for eight years I read, but never studied. I amused him, but never worked myself. I stood between him and a woman who wanted to become his stepmother ; and at the end of that time, at twenty-four years of age, I was cast adrift, with a fair library of books, and fifty pounds in my pocket. The poor fellow had left me all his mother's small property, four thousand pounds ; but there were such things said of me by that cruel woman, and Reginald's deluded father, that I flung the legacy to them, and, shaking the dust from my feet, left the house for ever. Mr. Worton would have had me back. He offered me money, he offered me any apology I chose to ask. He offered to 'advance my views;' but I cursed him and his patronage too, cursed the day he took me from my own station, and gave me a taste for luxuries I could never command.

"'You have had the best years of my life,' I finished ; 'you have unfitted me for work ; you

have made me as useless as if I had been born a
gentleman. You let them try to turn your son's
heart against me ; and when they failed in that,
you allow them to saddle his legacy with such
slanders as force me, for my own credit's sake, to
go out into the world a beggar, rather than be
beholden to the bounty of my dead friend. And
all for what ? All because a woman wants to
marry you ; all because you want an heir to Worton Court—an heir that I hope, and pray, and
believe will never be born to you. For God is
just, and He will not forget Reginald, and He
will not forget me.' "

"Hard words," said his auditor.

"They were too hard," answered Mr. Aggland,
—"too hard to speak to a misguided, childish old
man. I thought about them afterwards, till I
could bear the recollection no longer, and wrote to
apologise, to retract. Madam returned the letter,
with a note, stating that 'Mr. Worton appreciated
my present regret as highly as my former services ; and concluding want of money had procured him the honour of my communication,

inclosed me a cheque for a hundred pounds, the acknowledgment of which she begged might end the correspondence.' I sent back the cheque, and have since fought out my fight alone. What I have done during the years which have come and gone between this time and that could scarcely interest you. There are few things I have not tried my hand at; I have prospered in life, and was able moreover to keep my father without letting him take another sixpence from Mr. Worton; but it was hard work, beginning existence, as one may say, with soft hands—no profession, no useful learning—at four-and-twenty. Now, sir, you know why I do not desire patronage for my son—why I had rather see him earning his bread by the sweat of his brow than eating it, as I did, at a rich man's table. Going over my own story has made me see clearly that which is best for him; and I decline your offer, sir, though I thank you most heartily for it."

There was an awkward silence after this. Captain Stondon looked across at Skillanscar, and along the defile to the broken stone bridge, ere he began to say, in a voice so low that it almost seemed as though he were telling some secret which he feared being overheard—

"I have not been quite frank with you, Mr. Aggland. I wish to do something for Duncan, but I want much more earnestly to do something for myself. Will you aid me in the matter? May I count on your help?"

"What is it? What help do you need?" And the two men stopped and faced each other, seeing nothing for the moment but the shadowy future, which was coming towards them both as a reality and a substance, with giant strides across the hills.

"Can you not guess?" asked Captain Stondon.

"I would rather be certain," answered Mr. Aggland, drily.

"Well, then, it is this," said Captain Stondon, plunging desperately into his confession. "I want to marry your niece. I love her. I will try to make her happy; I will——"

"Stop a moment," interrupted Mr. Aggland, and he sat him down on a stone by the side of the path, and turned his face away from his companion, while he watched the hopes and the plans of his later life frustrated, the last fragment of his fancy castle levelled with the ground. If Phemie married this man she was lost to him and his. No matter how well Duncan got on in the years to come, Phemie might never be wife to him; there would be no cozy farm-house among the hills, to which he could wend his steps when the summer glory was lying on tree and grass and heather; there would be no ingle nook in the dark winter days to come, where he might be always sure of being greeted with looks of love and words of welcome. The doors of the modest house he had imagined for the pair were shut violently in his face. But for Phemie? while he stood without in the cold, there were other doors opened for her to pass through : she might be rich, she might become a great lady. Had he any right to stand between her and such a future ? Dare he condemn her to seclusion certainly, to poverty possibly ? Could he tell her to go afoot through life, whilst there was a carriage waiting to take her easily and pleasantly along the highways of a world, where struggles for daily bread and anxieties for the morrow were unknown?

Should he, for any selfish feeling—for any dread of losing her—for any personal consideration—stand between her and the prospect her beauty had opened out for her? Mr. Aggland thought he would try to be disinterested both ways: he thought he would try to forget, on the one hand, that if Captain Stondon married Phemie he should lose her, and he determined, on the other, that he would not sell the girl for any benefit likely to accrue to him or his from her change of position. He would think of Phemie, and Phemie alone. He would try to do his duty by her, and listen to all Captain Stondon had to say, quietly and dispassionately. Having made up his mind to which prudent course, Mr. Aggland turned to his companion, and said :—

"I was beginning to fear this; you perhaps think I ought to have seen it before, but I did not. Not even a suspicion crossed my mind until

Saturday night, and I have been trying ever
since to get rid of that suspicion. I mean nothing ungracious, sir; but I wish anybody else
rather than myself had picked you up from
there——" and Mr. Aggland flung a stone down
the path to the exact spot where Davy discovered
the traveller; "and I wish it had pleased you to
fall in love with any other girl in Cumberland
sooner than with Phemie Keller."

"You need not distress yourself about the
matter," answered the officer: "tell me to go,
and I will go. Though it would have been better
for me had you left me to die on the hill-side,
still, tell me to give up all hopes of future happiness, all chance of domestic contentment, and
I will do it. I will pay you for my life with my
happiness, and though the bargain be a hard one,
hold to it honestly."

"I believe you would," said Mr. Aggland, looking with a certain admiration at the man who
made this offer. "I believe you would. I believe
you to be honest and honourable, generous and
true, and that makes it all the harder for me to

say what I want to say.   I am between two stools
—I am on the horns of a dilemma—

> ' I am a heavy stone
> Roll'd up a hill by a weak child : I move
> A little up, and tumble back again.' "

"Let me speak first, then," suggested Captain
Stondon, seating himself as he spoke on a piece of
rock close by Mr. Aggland.   "Let me tell you I
have not run into temptation wittingly—that I
have not remained in your house, eaten your
bread, partaken of your hospitality, with any deli-
berate intention of frustrating your wishes, and
taking your niece from you.   Knowledge has
come upon me as it has come upon you, suddenly;
all I ask is for you to consider my proposal well
before you give me any answer.   I know what
you have desired; I know you want Miss Keller
to become your son's wife.   I see you have set
your heart on this match ; but I entreat you not
to prejudice her mind against me on this account.
I implore you not to influence her against me,
because you wish her to marry him."

Then Mr. Aggland tossed back his hair,—his

hair which was like the mane of a wild horse,— and said, "'Is thy servant a dog that he should do this thing?' Do you think I am 'moulded of such coarse metal' as all that comes to? Do you imagine I have no love for anything but myself —that, though I have reared her as my own child —though I do not deny that the idea of her leaving me, of her marrying you, is 'like the tyrannous breathing of the north,' which 'shakes all our buds from growing,'—that I cannot still desire her happiness, and try for her sake—for the sake of the dead and gone—to see clearly? I see two things: I see you can give her wealth and position; but——"

"But what?" asked Captain Stondon, as the farmer paused.

"She is little more than a child," said Mr. Aggland, hesitatingly, "and you are middle-aged."

"A man can love in middle age as well as in his earliest youth," answered Captain Stondon.

"True; but can a girl love that man?" asked the other. "I could not think of any one of Phemie's age except as a daughter, and I should say that you are as old as I am."

"If he only knew," thought Captain Stondon.

"It is too like May and December for my taste," Mr. Aggland went on, firmly. "She is in the very earliest springtime of life; she has got her April and May—her glorious summer-tide—all before her; and you, like myself, are travelling on towards the frosts and snows of winter. Is it a right thing, I ask you? I put it dispassion-ately—is it right?"

"Love takes no account of years," replied the officer.

"On the one side. I am talking of the other side. Phemie is but little over sixteen, and you are, say five-and-forty. Look at that, sir; thirty years—half a life-time—between you. Only think of it—thirty years at the wrong end; bad enough between thirty and sixty, but downright madness between twenty and fifty. And she will not be even twenty for more than three years to come! She is too young, sir, far and away too young."

"The difference is on the right side, replied Captain Stondon. "Does not your favourite Shakespeare advise—

> ' Let still the woman take
> An elder than herself ? ' "

"Yes; but I am not aware that Shakespeare advises a woman in any case to marry her father," retorted Mr. Aggland.

"She is older than Duncan, and you would have had her marry him," persisted Captain Stondon. "You would give her to him without a regret; you would shut her within the walls of this mountain prison for ever, and never sigh over such a waste of grace and beauty. You could see her working about her husband's house—working like a servant—and never wish she had been born to a different lot."

"You are wrong in some of your statements," answered Mr. Aggland; "yet she might be happy among these hills; and, if she were happy, I do not know that I ought to desire anything more for her. The Queen on her throne can be but that. If the peasant be happy, he is as prosperous a man as the peer; for happiness is the acme of earthly bliss. It is the Bathmendi of the Persian tale which we wander all over the world to find, while it lies awaiting us in some sequestered nook like Tordale."

Leaning his elbow on his knee, supporting his chin on his hand, Mr. Aggland looked thoughtfully and sorrowfully down the defile as he spoke.

All truth contains an echo of sadness; and it is for this reason, I suppose, because it is sad as well as solemn, that a man never speaks it either to his own heart or to his fellow without feeling graver for the utterance.

Some thought of this kind passed through Captain Stondon's mind even while he answered—

"Your argument will bear turning. A peer may be as happy as a peasant; the wife of a rich man as happy as the wife of a poor. If I have found my Bathmendi in Tordale, there is surely no reason why I should not carry it back with me to Marshlands. God knows I have waited long and travelled far.   Do not send me out again into the world—desolate."

And growing eloquent in the very extremity of his fear that he should be cast forth from this earthly heaven into which he had strayed all un-wittingly, Captain Stondon told the story of his life—of his cold, cheerless, lonely life—to his attentive auditor.   He told of the years he had lived unloved ; he spoke of the romantic affection of his boyhood—of the attachment he had che-rished—of the end which had come to it, and to all the dreams of his youth.   He told how he had never thought to love again—never thought to marry, or settle down, or hear the prattle of children, or look for an heir to all the broad acres of Marshlands.   As a man he appealed to a man. There was nothing he said with which Mr. Agg-land could not sympathise ; and, as he proceeded, the farmer began to see more and more that the match would be a good one for Phemie ; that if she could but love him, she had every chance of happiness.

A just man and a true, a faithful man and a

forbearing ; a man whose heart was as young as a boy's, who would be a husband, a lover, a friend, all in one ; who would feel for the girlish thing he was taking from among the mountains to the bustle and stir of the world ; who would take thought for her inexperience ; who would stand by her in trouble ; who would be staunch till death ; who did not consider love a light thing, or woman a toy, but who would take Phemie as a sacred trust, for the care of which he should have to answer before the throne of God.

And further—for it would be but half-telling a story to keep back any of the truth—Mr. Aggland could not be blind to the fact that, in a worldly point of view, Captain Stondon was a most excellent *parti*. He had thought his guest well-off, but he had never known *how* well-off he was, till the officer spoke at length of his position, of the value of Marshlands, of the nature of the settlements he could make ; of the extent of the property his son—if he had one—would inherit.

"I see," he said, at last, " that, putting aside the one obstacle, it would be a wonderful match for Phemie to make. Though she is well born, she has no fortune, and a pretty face is a poor substitute for a dowry anywhere. I know she will never get such an offer again, and if you can win her, wear her. Take her from us, for you can do better for her, I fear, than we can. The children will break their hearts to be parted from her, but that cannot be helped."

" Why should they be parted·? " asked Captain Stondon.

" Because, though Phemie has walked with us long," answered Mr. Aggland, " we have come to the cross-roads now, and her way lies different from ours. That is, it will lie different if she elect to go with you."

And, having uttered this sentence, which he spoke mournfully, the farmer rose to go back along the mountain path, cherishing no hope in his mind that Phemie would refuse her wealthy suitor, feeling a conviction that the girl would soon be leaving Tordale—leaving the old familiar scenes far behind her for ever.

But he did not interfere—he did not advise ;

there were plenty of people to tell her what a great match she might make, what a grand lady she might become, without his opening his lips on the subject. Gradually the neighbours began to talk. The young surgeon from Grassenfel twitted Phemie when he met her in the valley about having grown proud and distant. He supposed it was that fine gentleman lover of hers who had made her turn up her nose at humble suitors like himself. Then Mr. Conbyr threw out some hints in a decorous, clerical kind of manner, which showed that he evidently thought Miss Keller an amazingly lucky young person; not long after that, Duncan grew sulky, and Mrs. Aggland deferential; and Peggy, ay, even Peggy M'Nab, began to sound Captain Stondon's praises in her darling's ears.

Phemie had her senses. Phemie could not be blind—she knew what was coming; and when at last it did come, and she took counsel with her uncle, the pair cried in each other's arms, and then decided that Phemie should think the matter over, and give Captain Stondon an answer when she had thought it out quietly, and alone.

Sitting up in her little bed that night, with the ghostly white draperies looking still more white and ghostly in the moonlight, her head on Peggy's shoulder, her tears falling on Peggy's bosom, Phemie talked about Captain Stondon and his offer till she grew sick and weary. I think if Peggy had remained firm to the creed in which she was answerable for having brought her nurseling up, Phemie would scarcely have relinquished her dream husband without a greater struggle; but, as it was, Peggy turned traitor, and, in the face of reality, scouted the vision she had so often conjured up.

"I dare say he is very good," finished Phemie, "and I do like him very well; but he is not in the least like the lord you promised should come for me in a coach-and-four whenever I grew tall enough to be married."

"That was na' to be expectit," answered Peggy McNab, oracularly; and who may say but that Peggy's observation was strictly true? Perhaps

its very truth made the remark all the more irritating to Phemie, who, laying her head on her
pillow, cried herself to sleep, feeling that between
the romance of her life and the reality there was
indeed all the difference !

CHAPTER IX.

RETROSPECTIVE.

DURING the greater part of the next day, Phemie mended stockings as if her life depended on the rapidity with which she worked. She would not eat—she would not talk—she would not play with the children—but she would stitch on hour after hour, never lifting her eyes except to look out at the rain, which was pelting down in torrents.

Every one in the house knew as a matter of course that Phemie was making her choice ; even the youngest child contemplated her with a vague kind of wonder, dimly conscious that Phemie was thinking of something in which it could have no part or lot—something which separated her from the remainder of the household for the time being, which rendered it necessary for all conversation held in her presence to be unnatural and con-

L 2

strained, and which forced Daniel Aggland, junior
—the baby above mentioned—to sit down on the
carpet and stare at Phemie for a full half-hour
without winking.

There it sat, holding its shoeless foot with its
right hand, while sucking the thumb of its left—
there it sat, the child looking at the girl to whom
the woman's question, marriage, had come to be
solved so soon, until, having exhausted its wonder-
ment, it began to take offence at Phemie's un-
usual silence and at last burst out into a paroxysm
of indignant screams.

Then Phemie laid aside her work and comforted
it. She had grown so accustomed to nursing that,
young though she was, she could hush and quiet a
child's distress as cleverly as any matron in the
county. She had such a sweet voice, that instinctively the baby ceased crying to listen to its tones.
She had such a beautiful face, that the little
hands unclenched naturally in order to stroke it.
She had such divine hair, that infant eyes instinctively opened wide to watch the light flickering
and rippling over the braids.

She had such a way of gathering a child to her, that the tiny creature could not choose but lie still, nestling close to her heart. Dear Phemie Keller! pretty, vain, gay, fanciful, dreamy Phemie —thinking of you as you walked up and down that little sitting-room, hushing the child into quietness, it seems to me that Captain Stondon might well be excused for forgetting his own age and your youth, and remembering only the beauty which he saw, and the true, faithful nature that he had penetration enough to know you possessed.

"Poor baby Danny," muttered Mrs. Aggland *sotto voce*, as she watched the girl soothing the child's distress; "you won't have her long to coo over you and humour you at every turn; you'll be a poor forsaken baby soon, for mother won't have time to be waiting upon you as Phemie has done."

All of which Phemie heard, as Mrs. Aggland intended she should; truth being that Mrs. Aggland had a burning desire to know for certain what she was thinking about.

"It is the most unnatural thing I ever heard

of," said the mistress of the Hill Farm to Peggy M'Nab. "Instead of taking counsel with one and another, and being uplifted at the notion of being made a grand lady of for life, she sits like a statute mending them old stockings, not opening her lips to a soul, not even talking about her wedding clothes. Anybody might think it was sentence of death that had come instead of an offer of marriage."

"Marriage is an unco' serious thing," answered Peggy M'Nab.

"You may say that, Peggy," replied Mrs. Aggland; "not that you can know much about the matter from your own experience; but still it is not so serious a thing as a funeral; and Phemie sits there with as solemn a face as if she was at a burying, sighing every now and then as though her heart was like to burst."

"Maybe she's no on for taking him," suggested Peggy; "though he's weel enough, weel favoured and kindly spoken, he's no young, mistress. He's nearer a match for you or me, nor for such a bairn as Phemie."

"As for that, Peggy M'Nab," said Mrs. Aggland, "I will thank you to keep your distance, and not talk of your age and mine in the same sentence, when anybody with half an eye can see you might be my mother twice over."

"I would have had to begin young, then," remarked Peggy, parenthetically.

"And with regard to Captain Stondon," went on Mrs. Aggland, unheeding the interruption, "what does the few years' difference between him and Phemie signify? Won't she have everything she wants? Won't she have money, and leisure, and dress, and servants, and carriages and horses, and goodness only can tell what besides? And don't you know those are just the things Phemie has been hankering after all her life? Is she not the making of a fine lady?"

"She is bonny enough for one, at ony rate," put in Peggy.

"Some may think her so. I know I think her conceity enough for anything; and if she wants all this—if she wishes to be made a princess just at once, why need she look so miserable now

it is all put in her way—by the act of Providence,
as one may say ?   Does she think she will ever get
such a chance again ?   Does she think it snows,
and hails, and rains husbands on the hills ?   Does
she think a poor country girl can pick and choose
like some great heiress ?   Does she imagine all
the lords and dukes in the country are coming
down to Cumberland to make her a peeress out of
hand ?   If she thinks that, Peggy M'Nab, she is
mistaken, and so I tell you."

Nobody knew better than Peggy that Phemie
was mistaken.   Nobody knew better than the old
Scotch woman that there is deal of difference between a fairy tale and everyday life ; between the
lover of a winter evening's story and the suitor
who, in the broad daylight, comes in his proper
flesh and blood to ask for the fair maiden's hand.
Since the suitor had come across the hills—since
such astonishing good fortune had fallen to
Phemie's lot as to secure a real live gentleman for
her lover—Peggy M'Nab had seen light.   It was
very well to keep back the farmers' sons, and the
young tradesmen who sometimes came from the

neighbouring towns to see their parents at Tordale ;
but to reject Captain Stondon—to repulse this
middle-aged Robin Gray, when there was not a
Jamie at all in the question, Peggy saw would be
midsummer madness. Was not he, as she often
said, a " braw man," tall and erect, and gentleman-
looking, and of gentle bluid into the bargain ?
Had not he given her, Peggy, as much money in
one handful as she earned for wages in the course
of a year ? Was not he quiet spoken ? not a rant-
ing, shouting devil like the young surgeon from
Grassenfel, who alternately cursed Peggy for a fool,
and slapped her on the back, saying she was a great
old girl for all that. He did not drink spirits raw,
like Mr. Fagg. He did not come into the house
like a company of dragoons. You never heard
him say a wry word about his food ; whatever was
set before him he eat, let it be loaf-bread or oat-
meal, haggis or a joint. Was it not better to be
an old man's darling than a young man's slave ?
Spite of the fairy tales, and the lord's son, and the
carriage and four, was not Captain Stondon's offer
better than any reality Peggy had ever thought

likely to come in her nurseling's way? Vague visions are one thing—tangible success is another; and there is no use in denying that the tangible success which had come to Phemie Kéller astonished every person who knew that young lady, except, indeed, the young lady herself, who, having pacified the child at last, laid it down in its mother's lap, and then gathering up her work, went off to her own room, where, having locked her door, she drew a chair up to the window, and sat down to look out upon the valley of Tordale, whilst she thought of her own present—of her own future.

She was but a young thing after all, dear reader, to be thinking about the whole of her life to come —but a young, ignorant girl, to be brought in a moment face to face, with that which was to determine the weal or the woe of every future hour; and as she gazed down the valley her tears fell faster than the driving rain, and she leaned her head against the window-frame and cried as though her heart were breaking, at the choice she was called upon to make so suddenly.

It is not much to read about this man's mistake, about that woman's error; the book is closed, the tale forgotten, and the reader goes on his own path contentedly. Even when soul talking to soul some one tells his neighbour where and how he lost himself—how he went wrong—where he dug deep graves—where he laid down his heart in the coffin beside some frail human body, the listener, sympathizing though he may be, is apt to over-look what loss all this wrong and suffering involved.

Do you know when he has finished what it all meant? As he turns away, do you understand what he has been talking about? It was his life, man; and he had but one. But one, good God! and that is what none of these happy, prosperous people can be made to comprehend. He has spoiled his horn; he has not made his spoon. Other people have lives to live out and make the most of, but he has marred his: it may not signify much to you, my friend, but it signifies everything to him, because he cannot go back and begin *de novo;* it has been all loss, and in this world there

may never come a profit to compensate for that
which he has left behind.

Some idea of this kind, very vague and very
shadowy, passed through Phemie's mind as she sat
at the window looking through blinding tears at
the familiar landscape, at the mountains that had
been her friends for years. It might not be very
much she was considering; but it was her all,
nevertheless. Her little investment in the world's
great lottery might be a mere bagatelle; but it
was the whole of her capital, notwithstanding.

It was her life; it was what I have been trying
to talk about; it was everything she possessed of
value on earth, that she sat thinking of as the
evening darkness gathered down upon Tordale
church; upon the wet graves where the dead,
who had lived out their lives before she was born,
were sleeping quietly; upon the waterfall; upon
the trees; upon the distant valley; upon the
parsonage house, in the dining-room whereof Captain Stondon was standing at that very moment,
thinking, in the flickering firelight, of her.

As the seed-time is to the harvest; as the acorn

is to the oak; as the blossom is to the fruit, so was this vague thought to Phemie Keller, in comparison to what the same thought grew to, clear and tangible, in the after years, which were then all before her. It was instinct; it was an uncertain glimmering of an eternal truth. With the same shadowy indistinctness—with the same unreasoning terror as that of a child coming in contact for the first time with death—did Phemie Keller look out for the first time from her little bed-chamber on life.

Hitherto, though I have spoken of the promise of her beauty, I have said little of herself, and less of the kind of existence hers had been from childhood, until Captain Stondon met her in Tordale church. She is thinking of her past as she sits in the gathering darkness; thinking as she leans her head against the window-frame, and listens to the wind howling among the mountains, and the rain beating over the beautiful valley below—at one and the same moment of when she will be a woman, and of when she was a child. She is wondering, if she leaves Tordale, with what eyes she will look upon it again; what she will have to pass through, ere, in years to come, she returns to look upon it once more; and as she wonders, her memory casts back to the days that are gone, and she is a child in the old manse by the sea-shore, listening to the roar of the ever-restless ocean, lying in her bed with the waves singing her lullaby, wandering on the beach and building up palaces on the sand— palaces ornamented with shells, and set out with sea-weed that the next flood-tide destroyed!

What more did she see? what more did memory give back to her, as the waves cast up drift on the shore? Out of the past there came again to her the self she had been, the child she could never be more.

A child with a clear white skin, through which the veins appeared blue and distinct—a delicate child with a faint colour in her cheeks, with golden hair, who was mostly dressed in white, who had dainty muslin frocks, who had soft lace, edging her short sleeves, who was her grandfather's pet, who was the life and soul of the manse; with her old-fashioned talk; with her loving, clinging, twining, cheery, tender ways. A child who, being always with grown-up people, learned to think long before her proper time—a child who had never lain down to sleep when a storm was raging without praying God to bring those who were on sea, safe to land—a young thing who had seen women wringing their hands and mourning for the dead—who having lost both father and mother herself could understand the meaning of the word orphan, and cry with the fatherless children as they talked about the parents who might never again come home.

Right and wrong! She had learnt what both words signified in early days in that old manse by the sea-shore. From the time she could toddle, she had been wont to shake her head gravely at temptation, and to draw back her fingers from desired objects, lisping to herself, "Musn't; granpa's father in heaven wouldn't be pleased," and then she would mount on a chair, and, sitting cross-legged upon it, argue out the rest of the question to her own satisfaction.

There never was a better child than Phemie!
Save for the way she cried when the wind was
high, and the sea rough; save for the trick she
had of stripping herself half naked in order to
clothe any beggar brat who might happen to be
complaining of the cold; save for huffy fits she
took when her grandfather was too busy to notice
her; save for the unaccountable and unanswer-
able questions she was in the habit of propounding
suddenly—Phemie—little Phemie, I mean, had
not a fault.

The most terrible battle she and the household
at the manse ever fought was over the body of a
dead kitten, which she kept from decent burial
for a whole day, and which was at length taken
from her arms only when she had cried herself to
sleep over the loss of her pet. To grandfather
and servants, to the fishermen and their wives,
to the shepherds on the moors, to the children by
the roadside, Phemie Keller—little soft-hearted
Phemie—was an object of the tenderest interest
and affection.

The courtship of her father and mother was

talked of by the side of many a winter fire. The young things—boy and girl—who had fallen in love at first sight, who had met secretly by the sea-shore, who had been seen by the shepherds walking hand in hand together among the heather, who had wanted the old minister to marry them, and who had bound themselves together as man and wife before a couple of witnesses when he refused to let them wed unless the consent of the lover's family were first obtained, who had gone away out into the world together—all the story was repeated over and over whenever Phemie's name was mentioned in the lonely cottages scattered here and there through the thinly-peopled district.

The love-story with its sorrowful end; the love-story, finis to which was written on a moss-covered headstone in the quiet kirkyard close by! They had known her a girl, and she came back to them a widow—came back, "wi' her wee bit bairn, Phemie, to dee."

Was it not natural that a certain romance should be associated with Phemie in the minds of those who could remember her parents so well ? Was it to be wondered at, if they made, perhaps, too much of the child ; if they speculated as to her future lot, foolishly ?

Anyhow, Phemie was loved, and petted ; and never a princess ruled more absolutely over her subjects, than did the young child rule over the household at the manse. It was always who could please Phemie most, who could make her look prettiest, who could get sitting by her till she went to sleep, who could make time to take the child on her lap, and tell her the stories she liked best to hear.

All the old tales of fairies and brownies, of second sight, of witches and warlocks, were familiar to Phemie as her A B C. Old ballads were recited to her ; old songs were sung to her, till her head was as full of romantic narrative as it could hold.

There was not a blast that blew over the hills but touched an answering note in the child's heart. The poetry lying there always uttered some responsive tone in answer to the elements—

sunshine and shower, storm and calm, the wind whistling across the moors or sobbing through the fir-trees, the snow covering the earth, or the spring flowers decking the fields—all these things had a double meaning for Phemie; like a face reflected from glass to glass, every object in nature was projected into the child's heart from the heart of some one else who had basked in the summer glory, and braved the winter tempest before she was thought of.

Then came Death to the manse once more; and this time he took the old minister from among his people to the kirkyard, within sound of the mourning and murmuring sea. Thoughtful hearts tried to keep Phemie from seeing him in his coffin, but Phemie's thoughtfulness exceeded theirs.

Her love made her cunning; and then the episode of the kitten was repeated with the grief intensified, with the despair more terrible.

She was taken away to a friend's house, and kept there till the funeral was over. All the day they watched her; but at night, in the dead of

the winter time, she seized her opportunity and
tracked her way across the moors to the manse,
sobbing through the darkness as she toiled
along.

At the manse they watched her again, and
again she eluded their vigilance, and stole out
to the lonely kirkyard, where she was found
tearing up the wet mould with her little
hands; scratching at the newly-made grave like
a dog.

After that, grievous sickness—sickness almost
unto death, and then removal by slow stages to
the house of the only living relative willing to
receive her—Mrs. Aggland, her mother's sister.
The Agglands had children of their own; but
yet at the Hill Farm it was the old story enacted
once again by fresh performers. Her aunt could
not be too kind to her. Mr. Aggland might
punish his own daughter, but he never dreamt
of saying a cross word to Phemie Keller. She
was privileged : by reason of her desolateness, by
reason of her story, by reason of her sensitive
heart, that reproof and harshness would have

broken, Phemie had *carte blanche* to do as she
liked, and if she did not grow up indolent and
selfish, it was simply because there are some
natures that cannot be made indolent or selfish
by kindness and indulgence.

And yet it may fairly be questioned whether
Phemie would ever have developed into a useful
character, but for the death of her aunt. Whilst
Mrs. Aggland lived the girl had always some one to
think for her; see to her; love her. When once
her aunt died, out of very gratitude, for very pity,
Phemie was forced to think for others; see to
others; and give love, and care, and affection,
back.

"It was sic a sair sicht to see the puir maister
frettin' after his wife," as Peggy M'Nab asserted,
that by common consent Peggy M'Nab and Phemie
Keller joined together to make him feel his loss
in the trifles of every-day life as little as might
be. Phemie was still a child, a mere child, but
yet she could do something for the widower; she
could nurse the baby and keep its cries from
troubling its father; she could help Peggy in a

thousand little ways; she could amuse the little ones by repeating to them the stories she had heard told in broad Scotch, where the Scottish moors stretched away lone and desolate towards the north; she could read to him; she could work for him; she could stand at the door looking for his return; she could talk to him in the twilight; and she could make the sight of her bright pretty face as welcome to the solitary man as the flowers in May.

After his second marriage, Phemie proved more useful still. As she grew older, she grew not merely cleverer, but wiser—wise to hold her tonge, wise to keep unpleasantness in the background, wise to do the work she had to do with a cheerful countenance and a brave heart, wise towards everybody but herself, for she dreamed dreams and built castles all the day long.

Aided and abetted therein by Peggy M'Nab, who was never weary of telling Phemie about her father, about the great family he belonged to, about the grand folks, somewhere or other, with whom Phemie could claim kith and kin.

If Mrs. Aggland were cross, if Phemie wearied over her making and mending, if the girl ever took to fretting about the days departed, straight away Peggy told her nursling " to whisht."

"Canna ye quet yer greetin'—canna ye tak patience for a bit? Dinna ye ken that if ye wunna thraw that bonnie face o' yours, some braw laird will come ben when ye hae leest thocht o' him, and mak ye a gentle for life? He'll come in the gloamin' over the hills speerin' for ane Phemie Keller, and he'll tak ye awa', my bairn— he'll tak ye frae thrawn words and cross looks, and frae yer auld daft nurse wha canna bear to see ye forfoughten."

And then Phemie would declare she was not fretting, and that no laird, not even the Duke of Argyll himself, should take her from Peggy M'Nab.

"Wherever I go, ye shall go," Phemie was wont to declare; "and I'd like to take Duncan, and Helen, and the rest of uncle's children, and we could leave Mrs. Aggland her children, and make him come with us. Where should we go,

Peggy, and how should we go ? Tell me all about it."

Thus exhorted, Peggy would conjure up quite a royal procession for Phemie's edification.

With her darling's lovely head resting in her lap, with the girl's soft white fingers stroking her hard brown hands, Peggy was wont to talk of a hero so handsome and good and clever as to border on the impossible ; of estates and houses that might have made an auctioneer's fortune ; of furniture that sounded like an inventory taken· of the domestic goods and chattels of some establishment in fairyland; of horses that could never have been foaled on earth, so great was their speed, so extraordinary their beauty ; the crowning gem of the whole programme being the carriage, which, I am afraid, Peggy would have described as precisely similar to the state chariot of the Lord Mayor of London, had she ever been so blest as to behold that functionary's progress on the 9th of November through the City streets.

It was for long a vexed question between

Phemie and her nurse, whether the Kellers, or a distracted lover were to come for her.

Peggy held to the Kellers, but Phemie preferred the lover, who was to right her wrongs, to take her from the cinders, and dance with her at the ball, and get her the property of her ancestors, and live happily with her for ever after. She did not want to owe anything to her father's family. She preferred the idea of some dark-haired, dark-eyed nobleman coming to the Hill Farm like a flash of lightning, and rescuing her from stocking-mending and cast-off clothes, after the fashion of a hero of romance.

Sometimes in her fancy she would be proud and distant, sometimes indifferent, sometimes cruel and unkind; but however she began the story, it had never but one end, and that end was not suicide and distraction, but a grand wedding, and joy, and confidence, and love all the days of their lives.

They would build a castle on the site of the Hill Farmhouse, and come and spend some portion of every summer at Tordale. Mr. Conbyr

should have his organ, and she would bestow such
magnificent presents on the wives of the farmers
she had known! She would even give Mrs.
Aggland a satin dress, and a brooch, and a bonnet, and everybody should be happy, and all
should go joyous as a marriage bell.

As for the nobleman, he was to be something
between Fergus M'Ivor, the lover of the poor
Bride of Lammermoor, and Percy, as described in
Otterbourne. Whichever of these desirable models
he most resembled, there was yet one thing in
which he never varied—his devoted affection for
herself. Phemie experienced no pangs of jealousy: she had no mental misgivings about a pre-
vious attachment, about any former lady love. It
was to be first love with him as well as with her;
it was to be first love and last love with both.
Heaven help her! though these dreams may
sound worldly and calculating, they were nevertheless pure and innocent, and it was the shock
of coming down from the contemplation of such
a lover and such a fortune, to the flat level of
accepting or rejecting a middle-aged and unro-

mantic suitor that proved too much for Phemie's equanimity, and made her—sitting by the window looking down over Tordale valley—so sad and thoughtful.

For the touch of reality had done two things : it had wakened her at once from a land of pleasant visions, to the certainties of existence; it showed her she had been asleep and dreaming ; it proved to her she must wake and bestir herself.

She could not go on after this, picturing to herself the advent of an ideal lover. Like one arising from a long sweet slumber, she looked out over the plains of life, and saw her actual position for the first time.

She was born—not to be run after like a damsel of romance, but to darn stockings, and to be considered an amazingly fortunate girl if a rich prosaic man fell in love with and married her. She had overrated her goods ; she had been like a man with a clever invention, who never thinks of making hundreds out of it, but always millions, until some one offers him, say a thousand pounds,

with which all his friends consider he ought to
believe himself overpaid.

So long as her little possessions were kept out
of the market she placed a price on them far and
away above their actual value ; but now, when she
saw the precise sum at which she was rated by
other people, her spirits sank to zero.

If it were so wonderful a thing for this com-
monplace stranger to ask her to marry him, what
chance was there of the lord coming across the
hills to woo ?   Was it likely she should ever meet
Lord Ronald Clanronald by Strammer Tarn ?
And if she did meet him, was it at all probable
he would take her back with him to his home ?
Lizzie Lindsay had skirts of green satin, but
Phemie Keller had only three dresses in the
world, and none of them much to boast of !

Further, it was evident her uncle had laid her
out to marry Duncan.   He had mentioned it, and
she had told him that might never be.   Having
told him so, what was she to do—stay on mending old clothes and dreaming her dreams—dreams
that might never seem realities again—or go

away and become a lady, as every one told her she might by speaking only one word ?

Suppose, after all this to-do, after all this respect, after all this disturbance, she subsided again into the Phemie of six months previously, should she be able to lead the old life again patiently ? Could she endure Mrs. Aggland's scolding, and the incessant work, work, slave, slave, drive, drive, after this chance of freedom ? Suppose poverty came again : she had seen bad seasons at the Hill Farm, and felt the nipping of scarcity like the rest, and these bad seasons might return, and then, instead of being able to help, she would only prove an incumbrance.

If she accepted Captain Stondon, her hero would have to be turned with his face to the wall; but if she did not accept him, why, then, still the hero might never come, after all.

What should she do ? " Oh, what shall I do ?" sobbed Phemie, by way of a climax to her reverie; and, as if in answer to her question, Helen tapped at her cousin's door, and said :

" Captain Stondon is in the parlour, Phemie,

and father says, will you come down and see him ? "

."An' I hev brought ye up a candle, my bairn," added Peggy M'Nab; "redd up yer hair, and wash the tears aff yer face, for he'll no be pleased to see ye looking like a ghaist."

CHAPTER X.

THE grief must have been terrible, the anxiety intense, that could have made Phemie Keller indifferent to her personal appearance; and, accordingly, in spite of all her sorrow and indecision, the young lady took Peggy's advice kindly, and—followed it. She bathed her face, and then removed the traces of tears by breathing on her handkerchief and holding it to her eyes; she unfastened her hair, and let it fall down in thick luxuriant waves, which she combed and brushed caressingly.

She was very proud of her hair; her own beauty was a great pleasure to this mountain-reared maiden. Perhaps she would have been a more perfect character had she not taken such delight in her own loveliness; but then she would not have been Phemie Keller. She would not have been the girl who, full of innocent vanity, stood before her little glass, arranging her plaits and braids in the most becoming manner she could devise.

I have read a good many books, but I never recollect meeting in one of them with an account of a heroine who made herself look ugly in order to let down a rejected lover easily, nor among my own acquaintance have I ever known a woman forget, when discarding a suitor, to put on her best looks for the occasion.

It may be cruel, but is it not natural? Would you have Lesbia leave off her padding and stays, and her robe of gold, so that she might send the poor wretch away disenchanted? Would you have Nora Creina bind up her dishevelled locks, which are no doubt amazingly becoming to her, though they do not suit Lesbia, and put on a stiff robe of state, instead of the picturesque costume which floats as wild as mountain breezes, when she trips across the lea to say No, sir, no? Would you have Hebe push back her hair from her charming face, and make herself look a fright ? Would you have Miss, with the fine forehead and Roman nose, wear lackadaisical curls over her temples ? Would you have Drusilla uncover her scraggy shoulders, or Lavinia veil her snow-white neck ? Can you expect the dear creatures to send the man away, wondering at his own unutterable want of taste ? Is it not most natural that they should wish him to depart in a frame of mind bordering on insanity, possessed by seven fierce devils of loveliness, who make his last state worse by far than his first.

And finally, although the success she had achieved might not be that precise kind of success which Phemie's little heart desired to compass, was it not natural that, having gained a certain worldly triumph, auburn hair and dark-blue eyes should want to look their best over the matter ?

For all of which reasons, and more especially because the girl's vanity was as genuine as her grief, Phemie Keller brushed and smoothed and braided her hair as daintily as though she had been going down stairs to meet the hero of her dreams.

All women cannot go to the queen's drawing-room, though they may all wish to do so; but, spite of that, they put on their best dresses, and adopt the newest style of head decoration, when invited to a select tea-party at the squire's just outside the village.

Even for Mr. Fagg's benefit, even to gladden Mr. Conbyr's failing sight, Phemie would have made the best of herself, and as it was—so it was —this innocent, unsophisticated beauty took as much pains in arraying herself for the campaign as though she had been born and bred amongst those ancient ladies who wore tires on their heads and pillows to their arms, and went mincingly, making a tinkling as they went.

On the whole, the result was satisfactory. At sweet sixteen, tears are not altogether unbecoming. Rain, in the summer-time, produces a different effect on the landscape to rain in the winter; and, in like manner, it is one thing when tears wet the sweet buds of youth, and hang heavy on the roses of girlhood ; and quite another when they roll heavily down the worn cheeks of middle age, and mingle with the snows of later life.

All the sweeter did Phemie Keller look for the shower so lately fallen. There was a certain languor about her eyes, a certain pallor in her cheeks, which made her beauty irresistible; and as she turned to leave the room, the girl felt perfectly satisfied with her own appearance, and equally certain that Captain Stondon would be satisfied with it too.

And yet, spite of this conviction, there was a sick, faint feeling about Phemie's heart while she went slowly along the passage to decide her fate. How fearfully prosaic! how horribly matter-of-fact! how terribly real seemed this question which she was called upon to decide! There was no haze of love—there was no wild attachment—no passionate hero worship. She had never listened for his step with hand laid on heart to still its throbbings ; his voice had never sent the blood rushing to cheek and brow; she had never thought of him through the day, and dreamed of him by night; she had never walked with him hand-in-hand among the flowers of that enchanted garden which is the only Eden man ever now enters upon earth; the whispers of love were not in her ear, urging her footsteps on. It was a hard, cold bargain, and though Phemie did not, could not reason all this out for herself, as I have done for you, reader, still she instinctively hung back, and delayed the evil moment as long as possible.

"I am going down now, uncle," she said, opening the door of Mr. Aggland's private sanctum, a room filled with books, ornamented with fire-arms, littered with fishing-tackle, into which none of the household were privileged to enter excepting Phemie herself. "I am going down now," and she stood in the doorway, looking as if she never wished to go down, but wanted to stay there for ever; while Mr. Aggland, who was busy among the pipes of the organ referred to on one occasion by Mr. Conbyr, lifted his head, and bade her come in.

"I do not tell you to do anything, Phemie," he said; "remember that," and he laid his hand on her shoulder while he spoke. "So far as I see, you need not even make up your own mind just at present. Do not be in a hurry to say either yea or nay. 'Hasty marriage seldom proveth well,' Shakespeare says, as you know, and further—

'What is wedlock forcèd, but a hell,
An age of discord and perpetual strife?'

For which reason, do not let anyone over-persuade you in this matter.

'For marriage is a matter of more worth
Than to be dealt in by attorneyship.'"

"I know as much about my mind now as I shall ever know," answered Phemie. "I have been thinking, thinking all day, till I am sick of thinking. Advise me, uncle," she added, with sudden vehemence; "tell me what I ought to do."

"Seneca says—" began Mr. Aggland.

"Oh! never mind what Seneca says," interrupted Phemie; "I want to hear what you say."

"Well, then, my opinion is exactly his," persisted her uncle; "that no man should presume to give advice to others who has not first given good counsel to himself."

"You are playing with me," she said, pettishly. "I want advice, and you give me old saws instead: I want help, and you will not hold out a finger towards me."

"Because I cannot," he answered. "You are coming for advice to a man who, never having followed any rule of reason in his own life, is incompetent to show the wisest course to another. I have been led by impulse for so long that I believe I have forgotten there is such a thing as prudence. All my life long I have lacked 'good sense;'

'Which only is the gift of heaven ;
And though no science, fairly worth the seven.'

It was but the other day I was reading what William Finlay wrote about himself, and I thought then that the picture might have been drawn from me."

And Mr. Aggland hummed—

" ' While others have been busy bustling
After wealth and fame,
And wisely adding house to house,
And Baillie to their name ;
I, like a thoughtless prodigal,
Have wasted precious time,
And followed lying vanities,
To string them up in rhyme.' "

"Uncle, if you asked me for anything, I would give it to you," said Phemie, reproachfully.

"And so would I give you anything but advice," he answered.

"Anything except what I want," she said— "anything but that;" and at the words, Mr. Aggland rose up, startled.

"Phemie, child," he exclaimed, "do you know what it is you are asking from me ? do you think what it is you want me to decide ? It is your future; it is the whole of that which I once owned, but which is now behind me for ever; and I have made such a wretched thing of life, that I cannot tell you what to do. I am no judge, my dear; I am no judge."

"But I have nobody else," she said, piteously, "and I cannot keep him waiting all night, and I do not know what to say, and—and my heart is breaking." At which point, Phemie's composure gave way, and she covered her face with her hands and sobbed aloud.

"Damn marriage !" was Mr. Aggland's remark, and he uttered it in all sincerity. "I wish we were in heaven, Phemie, where there is neither marrying nor giving in marriage; where there are no bad crops, and no anxieties concerning the future. I cannot advise you whether or no to take Captain Stondon's offer; but I do advise you to hear what he has got to say about the matter. He is a good man, and a true:

> ' Nature might stand up
> And say to all the world, this was a man.'

You may find some one whom you could love better, Phemie, but you would never find anybody better. And, because I believe this, I bid you go and listen to him first, and afterwards, if you like, we will talk together."

And with this safe counsel, having dismissed his niece, Mr. Aggland turned him to his work again, muttering Otway's opinion, "'The worst thing an old man can be is a lover.'"

It was not the worst thing imaginable, however, for Captain Stondon; it was well for him to have an object given to his objectless life; well for him to have some one to think of beside himself; well for him to have at last a definite hope in existence:

and sitting all alone by the fire, the officer was dreaming some pleasant dreams, and thinking himself far from unfortunate, when Phemie turned the handle of the door and entered shyly.

But as she did so—as she came slowly out of the darkness into the light, something like a shadow seemed to come out of the darkness more swiftly than she and stand between them. It was not a doubt, and yet Captain Stondon felt himself remain irresolute for a moment; it was not fear, and yet he had experienced the same sensation before entering a battle from which he had been afterwards carried wounded : it was a cloud thrown for a moment over a landscape, fair to see, lovely to contemplate ; it was one of those intangible messengers of evil who, fleet of foot, rush through our hearts in the midst of our joy, bidding us prepare for the sorrows that are following more slowly after into our lives.

It just came between them for a moment and departed, and next instant Captain Stondon was holding the girl's hands in his, and praying her forgiveness for his over-haste. In one sentence he told her, he had not been able to rest at the vicarage; that he could not sit patiently waiting to hear his fate: in the next, he begged her to believe he was in no hurry; that he would not hasten her decision; that whenever she chose to give him an answer, would be the time he should like best to hear it.

"All this day," he went on, "I have been thinking of you. I have been longing to be at the Hill Farm once more. I have been wishing for the sound of your voice. I know I ought not to have come here this evening; but I could not live without seeing you. Do not say anything to me if you would rather not. Send me away again now, and I will go through the darkness and the rain, content to have looked in your face once more."

It was needful for him to do all the talking, for Phemie never opened her lips. She never helped him in the least, but stood with one hand resting on the stone chimney-piece, looking intently into the fire. If she had been born deaf and dumb, she could not have made less sign, and yet still all the time she was struggling to find words to tell him what was passing through her heart; she was trying to discover what she was feeling, so that she might show him honestly all that was in her mind.

He might not be a hero, but he loved her; he might not have black hair and piercing eyes, but he was not beyond the pale of humanity on that account. All the strength of feeling—all the power of affection he had never, since his earliest youth, lavished on any human being, he was now wasting upon her, as the sea lays its treasures upon some bare and thankless strand: and even as the waves of that same sea, meeting some tiny stream, force back the waters of the rivulet and prevent it mingling with the ocean, so, the very force and vehemence of this man's passion stopped Phemie's utterance and made her shrink back into herself.

She felt as one standing out unsheltered in a hurricane—she felt powerless to speak—to lift up her voice and protest against marrying him solely because he wished to marry her. She felt what many an older woman has felt—that she had got into a mess, out of which it was impossible to extricate herself. Through no wish—through no striving—through no desire of her own—this man had fallen in love with her, and she would never have the courage to bid him go : she could do nothing but what she did do—lift her lovely, pleading eyes to his and burst into tears.

Then he knew—then the shadow fell between them again—then he paused before he took the girl gently to him and soothed her grief, and calmed her agitation as though he had been her father. He had deceived himself; he had thought this young thing could love him; he had thought, because he was still able to feel affection, that the power of winning the heart of a creature in her teens was left also. He had remembered his lands and his houses, his gold and his silver; but he had forgotten what mere gewgaws these things seem in the eyes of a girl unless she has some one dearer to her than aught else on earth—to hold and to spend with her.

He had deceived himself, and he awakened to the knowledge with a pang, and then straight away he fell to deceiving himself again, and thought that if once he could get her to say yes —if once he could induce her to marry him— he would earn her love; he would purchase it by his tenderness, by his forbearance, by his devotion.

Anything rather than give her up—anything sooner than lose auburn hair and blue eyes for ever—any trouble—any sorrow—any pain—if trouble, sorrow, and pain, could hinder his going out again into the wide world without Phemie Keller by his side.

And never had Phemie seemed so charming to him as she did at that moment; never in her gayest mood had he loved her so much as he did when she stood there passive, letting him stroke her hair, and draw her hands away from her tear-stained face, as though she had been a child.

Everything which strikes us as most beautiful in girlhood adorned Phemie Keller then: innocence, timidity, dependence, guilelessness—the man could have knelt down and worshipped her. She was so young, so fresh, so lovely, so different from anything he had ever seen before, that Captain Stondon felt his pulses grow still as he looked at her—felt the spell of her purity and beauty laid upon him soothingly.

He could not give her up; he told her so more calmly than he had spoken any sentence yet. He knew that in many respects he was not the lover to win a young girl's fancy, but he would prove none the worse husband for that.

She should have as long a time as she liked to think the matter over; he would not hurry her; the winds of heaven should not breathe upon her too roughly if she married him; they would travel. He would take her to Paris and Rome; they would go to Switzerland and Spain. She should see all the places of which she had read. He would make her uncle's position more comfortable.

Duncan should be sent to school, and Helen also; and Helen should come and spend her vacations at Marshlands. As for Phemie, if his love, if his care, if his wealth, if his devotion could keep trouble from crossing her path, life should to her be but as a long pleasant summer's day; and then Captain Stondon went on to tell her how he had never loved but once before, and of what a desert his life had been since.

"But you can make it a heaven upon earth now, if you will," he said; "you can make me either the happiest or the most miserable of mortals."

Yet still she never spoke.

"Am I to go away without one word?" he said. "Will you not say anything to me before I return to the vicarage?"

But Phemie never answered.

"Am I to take silence as consent so far?" he went on.

In answer to which question the girl remained resolutely mute.

"May I think that you are not averse to me?" he persisted; but the sweet lips never opened, the lovely face never was turned towards him.

"Do not send me away without even a smile," he said at last. "Well, well, I will not teaze you," and he made a feint of turning to leave the room.

Then all at once Phemie found words, and cried—

"Do not go, Captain Stondon; I want to speak to you. I have something to say—do not go!"

"Nobody will advise me," went on the girl, passionately: "if I was to inquire of any person I know, what I ought to do, they would tell me what I could tell them; that you have done me a great honour; that it is a wonderful thing for a gentleman like you to have asked a girl like me. I went to my uncle, and he bade me come to you; and I do come to you, sir. What am I to do? oh! what am I to do?"

It was his turn to be silent now, and he stood looking at Phemie, at her clasped hands, at her beseeching attitude, at her eyes which were swimming with tears, for a minute before he answered—

" My poor child, how can I tell you what to do ? I, to whom ' yes' will be life, and ' no' death, to every plan and hope, and desire of my future existence. All I can say is, do not marry me if you think it will not be for your happiness to do so ; and, above all, do not marry me if you care for anyone else."

He put such a constraint upon himself as he said this, that Phemie, though she caught their sense, could scarcely hear his words.

She did not know anything of the storm which was sweeping through his heart ; but she had a vague idea that he was fighting some kind of battle when he went on—

" I love you so well that you will be safe in making me your friend. If anyone else is fond of you, if you are fond of any other person, tell me, and I must try to be disinterested—try to see my duty and do it. Have you any attachment—any preference ? Answer me frankly, dear, for God's sake, for it may save us both much misery hereafter."

The pretty head drooped lower, and the flushed

cheeks grew redder; but the sweet lips parted for all that, and Phemie whispered—" No."

" You are certain ? " he said, and he raised her lovely face, so that he might see the story it had to tell.

This time Phemie lifted her eyes to his shyly, yet trustingly, while she replied—

" I am quite sure, sir—quite."

That was a comfort, at any rate : terrible jealousy of Mr. Fagg—grave doubts concerning one or two young men he had met in the valley— suspicions of some secret lover, whose very exist- ence was unknown to anyone but Phemie—had all conspired together to make the officer's life a weariness to him during the last few minutes; but there was no mistaking Phemie's face and Phemie's manner. She had no clandestine attachment—no attachment of any kind—not even for him.

There was the misery—there was the next difficulty he had to face, but Captain Stondon did face it for all that, and said—

" I am afraid that you do not care for me ?"

"I do not know, sir." What an aggravating chit it was with its uncertain answers—with its frightened manners and averted face !

"Do you dislike me, Phemie ?"

"No, sir."

It was on the tip of Captain Stondon's tongue to say, "Then what do you do?" but he refrained, and proceeded: "Could you learn to love me ?"

"I do not know;" and the officer struck his heel impatiently against the floor at her reply.

What was the use of catechising her thus ? What is the use of asking a child who does not know its A B C, questions about reading, writing, and arithmetic ? And was not all the alphabet of love a terra incognita to Phemie Keller ? Like a baby, she knew fairy tales; but she was ignorant of her letters. Practical love was a thing of which she knew as little as chubby five-years-old knows of Hebrew. The right master to teach her had never crossed her path; and though Captain Stondon was perfectly up in the subject himself, he lacked the power to impart information to her.

She might marry him—she might be fond enough of him—she might bear him sons and daughters; but she could never feel for the husband she was bound to—love, such we mean when we talk about "The dream of Life's young day."

It was natural, however, that Captain Stondon should blind himself to this fact—natural that, loving her so much, he should forget everything except that she was free—that it was possible for him to gain her—that he might hope to see her mistress of Marshlands yet.

He might win this young thing for his wife; and as he thought of this—thought it was only her youth which made her answers vague—her inexperience which caused her uncertainty—his impatience vanished, and sweet visions arose of an angel walking side by side with him upon the earth. He saw her flitting from room to room in the great house that had always hitherto seemed to him so deserted; on the lawn, in the gardens, he beheld blue eyes and auburn hair—pleasant pictures of home-life—home-life, such as he had often read about in books, were before his eyes; that which he had dreamed of so many, many years before was all coming true at last. She did not dislike him: for the rest—"She did not know." He would be satisfied with that for the present; and instead of pressing the unsatisfactory part of the subject, he would talk to Phemie about what she could understand, viz., her position as Mrs. Stondon, in comparison to her position as Miss Keller.

Wherein Captain Stondon was wise. Phemie possessed as much common sense as her cousins. Setting the lord out of the question, and putting the Kellers along with the lord, she knew exactly how she was situated to a T; and if the officer did put the actual state of matters in plain English before her, Phemie had quite sufficient knowledge to understand that all he said contained neither more nor less than the truth.

Mr. Aggland was not rich. If he died—and Phemie had seen enough of death to convince her

disease might visit the Hill Farm any day—the
girl would have no home, no friends, no money.
Or if sickness came—sickness and bad seasons—
how were the family to be supported ?

Again, if all went well, did she think she could
be content to spend all her life in Cumberland ?
Would she not like to go abroad, to mix in society,
to have plenty of money with which to help her
relations, and to repay some portion of what had
been done for her ?

As a man of the world, Captain Stondon could
not but know that the match would be a capital
one for Phemie ; and though he would have given
all he possessed ten times over cheerfully to get
her for his own, he still placed his social advantages in their best light before her.

And Phemie listened, and Phemie thought, and
the longer she listened and the more she thought,
the stronger grew the idea that she should marry
this man—that she would be somehow throw-
ing away her best chance if she refused to take
him.

She did not like saying Yes ; and yet she was

afraid the day might come when she would rue saying No. He was very good—he was very patient—he was very kind—he was very generous —why should she not be happy ?

If an infant be crying its eyes out, a skilful nurse has but to dangle a bunch of beads before it, and straightway the tears are dried, the sobs cease, and with a crow of delight feeble little hands are stretched out to seize the glittering prize.

Somewhat after the same fashion, Phemie Keller had been crying for that which she could not get; and now, partly because she was weary of weeping, and greatly because the world's vanities looked tempting as Captain Stondon presented them for her contemplation, she gra- dually forgot to shed any more tears, and began to listen with interest to what he was saying.

He told her about Marshlands—about its fine timber, about its old-fashioned rooms, its endless corridors, its lovely gardens.

Carriages, horses, visitors, servants—all these things, which are doubtless as valueless to you, my reader, as the string of beads are to the adult, looked very tempting to Phemie Keller.

She had not been used to such vanities, and people who have not known luxuries are apt to overrate the happiness of their possession. By degrees she began to ask questions, and to listen with interest to his answers; almost imperceptibly she came to see that, though Captain Stondon might not be a lord, he was a grand personage— a wealthy gentleman for all that. He was doing her an honour, and a man has travelled a long way towards success when he makes a woman feel this.

"He could get many a great lady to marry him," thought Phemie, and she felt grateful to him for choosing her. He would give her money to buy toys for the children—a microscope or a telescope for her uncle, and a gown for Peggy McNab.

She would have to darn no more stockings, but he would very probably let her get as much Berlin wool and canvas as would enable her to work a sofa-pillow like one there was down at the Vicarage. She should go to London, and perhaps

see the Queen. Altogether, she did not feel so
very miserable after he had been talking to her
for half-an-hour, and though she was still resolute
not to say Yes in a hurry, she promised to speak
to her uncle.

Of course Captain Stondon knew by this time
that her consent was a mere question of time.
His wooing might be tedious, but it could not be
difficult ; and as he took his way down the valley,
he found himself thinking about the marriage
service, and picturing to himself how exquisite
Phemie would look as a bride.

Ere a week was over, she had promised, re-
luctantly possibly, but still faithfully, to become
his wife some day; and the officer went about in a
seventh heaven of ecstacy, whilst Mr. Aggland sat
gravely looking on, and Duncan sang in a broad
Scotch dialect, which was fortunately unintelli-
gible to the lover, though Phemie understood it
all too well—

" He wandered hame wearie—the nicht it was drearie,
    And thowless he tint his gate 'mang the deep snaw ;
  The owlet was screamin', while Johnnie cried, ' Women
    Wad marry auld Nick if he'd keep them aye braw.' "

CHAPTER XI.

HAVING won Phemie Keller, the next thing Captain Stondon desired was to wed her. It might have made the heart of many a match-making mother ache with envy to hear how the man hammered on at that one string.

It was the refrain of every sentence. Mr. Agg-land and he never separated without the subject being mooted by this fortunate lover. Vainly did the farmer assert that the girl was too young, that there was time enough, that nobody was going to run away with her. Captain Stondon would listen to no objections. Christmas was coming on, and he must get back to Norfolk immediately, and he wanted to have something definite decided on before he went away.

To all of which Mr. Aggland listened gravely ere he replied—

"Then I tell you what, Captain Stondon : let me go to Norfolk with you, and there we will talk about the future. You must not think," proceeded Mr. Aggland, hastily, "that because I say this I am 'a kind of burr—I shall stick.' I do not mean to intrude. I have no intention of forcing myself upon you. Once let me see the place where Phemie is going to, the home in which she is to live, and you need never fear sign or token of me again."

"But I hope and trust that I shall," answered Captain Stondon: "I do not want to separate Phemie from her friends. I have no wish to do anything of the kind. You surely have not thought me so forgetful—so ungrateful as all that comes to ?" cried the officer, growing quite vehement over the matter.

But Mr. Aggland shook his head and answered, "I do not think you either ungrateful or forgetful, only I know that, when once you and Phemie are married, the less she and you are troubled with any of us the better it will be for her. It is never a pleasant thing for a woman to be constantly reminded whence she has been transplanted, and Phemie is young enough to take kindly to a new soil and root herself firmly in it. Further, sir; though I was once humble companion to a gentleman's son, I hope I never wore

> ' The rags of any great man's looks, nor fed
> Upon their after meals.'

And because I am so sure of my own mind in this matter—so positive that I do not want Phemie to feel anyone belonging to her a burden, I have no scruple in asking you to let me go to Norfolk. I shall be able to give her away with a lighter heart when I have once looked on the house that is to be her home."

Doubtless Mr. Aggland was right; but Captain Stondon, with his heart full of generous projects, with a vivid memory of all he owed to the farmer's care and kindness, felt that this constant assertion of independence—this everlasting refusal to come up and stand on the same level with himself—was irritating in the extreme.

It is so hard to have one's best intention doubted—to see people thinking they are wiser and better than everybody else on earth—to have good gifts tossed back in one's face, that Captain Stondon often felt inclined to tell Mr. Aggland that independence may be carried far too far; that there is an extreme point at which every virtue touches a vice; and that the most dangerous pride is, after all, the pride that "apes humility."

But as often as he felt inclined he refrained. He remembered that, to a man like Mr. Aggland, poverty was the most severe trial to which his character could have been subjected; and he recollected likewise that, if an ungenial climate had made the fruit of his life somewhat bitter, it had not rendered it unwholesome.

Besides, he, Captain Stondon, was so happy that he could afford to be tolerant of the shortcomings of others; and accordingly he answered, good-humouredly—

"You will know me better some day, Aggland. Meantime, come to Norfolk, and we can arrange about settlements and other matters when once we get there."

"One thing more," said Mr. Aggland. "I pay my own expenses."

"Agreed," replied Captain Stondon, laughing; "so long as you do not ask me to send you in a bill for board and lodging at Marshlands, you can pay what you like."

And so the matter was settled; and for letting Mr. Aggland have his own way the officer received his reward.

Never had the Hill Farm been made pleasanter to him than it was during the week which intervened between the time the journey was proposed and the hour they started.

Everyone seemed now to feel that matters were finally settled, and that there was, therefore, nothing more to be done except to put on holiday faces, and make matters agreeable for Phemie and Captain Stondon.

What if the boys did tease their cousin? It only made a little more life about the Farm. What if Johnny King had the audacity to answer

Captain Stondon's question as to whether
Mr. Aggland was at home with a wink and
a shrug, and a hand pointed over his shoulder,
and

"No, he is not; but Phemie is in there; and
father says she is all you want at the Hill Farm!"
The officer only boxed the young monkey's ears,
and went on his way with a light step, whilst
Phemie's whole time was taken up in expostula-
ting and remonstrating.

"Uncle, are they to torment me? Uncle, is
Duncan to say the things he does? Is he to go
about the house singing, 'Woo'd, and married,
and a'?'—more particularly when Captain Stondon is here. It is enough to put a person from
being married at all."

"The lassie is glaikit wi' pride," remarked
Duncan, from a safe distance.

"The Lord has been very good to her to put
such a chance in her way," added Mrs. Aggland,
sanctimoniously.

"Blest if I don't think Phemie is right, and
that it is enough to prevent her marrying at all,

hearing so much about it," said Mr. Aggland ; but
for all that the boys would teaze, and Mrs. Aggland would talk concerning the wedding-clothes,
and Peggy M'Nab would spend hours tracing out
a brilliant future for her darling. On the whole,
that future was by no means one to be scoffed at
by a country girl whose entire fortune was under
a couple of hundred pounds, and whose well-born
relations refused to recognise her. It was very
pleasant to become in a moment a person of importance—very charming to be the sun round
which the whole household revolved—very de-
lightful to have Mrs. Aggland alternately fawn-
ing upon her and making envious speeches.

Already Phemie was beginning to feel the
beneficial change in her position, and from the
height she had attained she was able clearly to
see the inferiority of the station from which Captain Stondon had raised her. Distant, and more
distant still, grew the heroes of her romantic
visions. They were real men to her no more ;
and she could even smile to herself as she repeated a verse of Carrick's " Rose of the Canon-

gate," a song she had learned in the old manse by
the sea-shore :—

> " She dream'd of lords, of knights, of squires,
>   And men of high degree ;
>   But lords were scarce and knights were shy,
>   So ne'er a joe had she."

Perhaps a letter Mr. Aggland received from her
aunt, Miss Keller, in answer to one he wrote in-
forming the Keller family of Captain Stondon's
proposals, and Phemie's acceptance of them, had
a little to do with this desirable change in her
sentiments. " Miss Keller presented her compliments to Mr. Aggland, and on behalf of herself
and her brother, General Keller, begged to inform
Mr. A. that they were happy to hear the young
person referred to in his letter was likely to be
comfortably provided for. At the same time, as
Lieutenant Keller's unhappy marriage had severed
all ties of relationship between them, General and
Miss Keller trusted that Mr. Aggland would not
think it necessary to enter into any further correspondence, as it was impossible for either General or Miss Keller to recognise in any way the
child of such a degrading and ill-assorted union."

"Never mind, my darling," said Captain Stondon, when Phemie showed him this gracious epistle. "You can do without them, I hope;" and the girl was grateful for the tone in which the words were spoken, and thought more and more that things were not so bad as they seemed at first, and that she had great cause for thankfulness.

She had to keep a guard on her lips and refrain from wishing for anything, for so surely as she said she would fancy this, or something else, so surely it was purchased for her. If she had expressed a desire for the moon, Captain Stondon would straightway have set to work thinking how he might best procure it; and Phemie could often have bitten a piece off her tongue after she had exclaimed—

"I should like this. I wish I had that."

"It seems as if I were always taking—taking, and I cannot bear it," she said once, piteously; and Mr. Aggland coming to the rescue, said he could not bear it either.

" The girl will forget how to say any other word

than 'thank you,'" he added; "you are making a perfect parrot of her. Give her what you like when once she is your wife, but hold your hand now;" and Captain Stondon agreed to do what they asked him on condition that the Norfolk journey was undertaken without delay.

"When once she is my wife she shall not need to wish," he said; from which speech it will be seen that Phemie's future husband had laid himself out to spoil her completely, if he could; and meantime he made so much of her—was so patient, so good, and kind, that Phemie, poor child, cried when he went away, and caused the man to fall more rapturously in love with her than ever.

If the weather had been better, the journey to London could have left nothing to be desired; but as it was, with the snow on the ground, Captain·· Stondon acknowledged to himself that, but for Mr. Aggland, he should have found the way between Carlisle and Euston Square of the longest.

Having Mr. Aggland, the time passed rapidly enough. They talked a good deal, they slept a good deal; and by-and-by, when they both awoke about Stafford, Mr. Aggland roused himself thoroughly, and began to show his companion what really was in him.

He told tales of his own long-ago : his boyhood's scrapes, his manhood's chances, the various adventures he had met with in the course of an irregular rambling life. The excitement of travelling, the sight of so many strange faces, the change and variety of going back after years to London, seemed to make a different creature of the individual who had always hitherto seemed to Captain Stondon a clever, eccentric "wild man of the hills."

"If he would but shave himself and get his hair cut, and buy a respectable suit of clothes, he might pass anywhere," thought the officer ; but he would as soon have dreamed of suggesting any alteration in his attire to the Commander-in-Chief as to Mr. Aggland, for which reason, though every one they met, stared at the man as they might at a maniac, Captain Stondon appeared perfectly unconscious of the fact ; and for any remark he made, Phemie's uncle might have been "got up"

like the greatest dandy that ever walked down
Bond Street.

Only—he told the cabman to drive to an hotel
in the City instead of to the "Burlington," where
he usually stopped, alleging as his reason that he
wanted to be near the Shoreditch Station, so as
to get on to Norfolk betimes the next morning.

When the next morning came, however, Mr.
Aggland asked whether his companion would object to putting off their journey for a few hours.

"I see," he said, "there is an afternoon train
which arrives at Disley about nine o'clock in the
evening. If that would suit you equally well, I
should prefer it."

"I have no objection," answered Captain Stondon. "I must telegraph down, though, for them
to meet us at the nine train, for otherwise I do not
see exactly how we should ever get over from Disley
to Marshlands."

"Thank you," said Mr. Aggland; "and would
you—would you—mind my leaving you alone for
a short time?"

The man actually coloured as he asked this

and after he had departed, Captain Stondon fell to wondering where his companion could be gone —on what secret mission he could have departed by himself.

"He surely has not seen some pretty woman and fallen in love with her," soliloquised the officer; and then his thoughts went back to the pretty girl he had fallen in love with in Cumberland, and whom he hoped to have all to himself when next he passed through London.

How little he expected, when he was in town before, ever to marry—ever to see anybody again for whom he could care in the least; and now he was lying on a sofa in one of the sitting-rooms in the Castle and Falcon, building all kinds of beautiful edifices, while the City traffic thundered along Aldersgate Street, till finally, with its very monotony, it lulled him to sleep.

How long he slept he did not know, but at last he awoke with a start, and found a stranger sitting opposite to the sofa he occupied—a stranger, yet not a stranger—a person who was unknown to him, and yet whose face seemed familiar. Cap-

tain Stondon raised himself on his elbow to inquire who his visitor might be, but in the same
moment recognised him, and exclaimed—

"Good heavens, Aggland! what have you been
doing to yourself? I could not, for the life of
me, think who you were."

And indeed it was no marvel that Captain
Stondon had been mystified; for Mr. Aggland
who entered the Castle and Falcon at one o'clock
was certainly remarkably unlike the Mr. Aggland
who walked out of it at eleven. He had gone to a
hair-dresser's, he had gone to a tailor, and the consequence was that he came back another person.
Hitherto his head had looked like the wings of an
old raven that is moulting; now dexterous hands
had brushed and smoothed his hair till it seemed
really to be human hair, and not the mane of a
wild colt. His moustache had been as the bristles
of a well-worn hearth-broom; and heaven only
knows through what torments of fixatrice he had
passed in order to get it into decent trim. His
whiskers had resembled nothing so much as long,
bare, straggling branches of the hop plant; but

the barber's skill having pruned away all the impoverishing suckers, the original hair on his cheeks remained trim and neat as could have been desired.

At his clothes Captain Stondon stared in amazement. About the legs and shoulders, about his feet and arms, Mr. Aggland was now as other men.

Excepting that he still wore his shirt-collar turned down—a fashion which in those days was not in vogue—the farmer looked quite like ordinary mortals. He had compassed that metamorphosis which Captain Stondon so earnestly desired to see ; and having compassed this end, it is only fair to add that Mr. Aggland looked desperately ashamed of himself.

But he had thought it right to give heed to such vanities for Phemie's sake ; and a sense of duty consequently supported him through his trial.

" I did not care to go to your place looking an old guy," he explained, awkwardly enough ; " and as I should have had, sooner or later, to buy a few things for the wedding, I have bought them sooner instead of later—that is all."

" You do my place too much honour," answered Captain Stondon ; but he wished, even as he said it, that he could be quite sure Mr. Aggland had not guessed what was passing through his mind as they journeyed southward together.

He had forgotten what keen vision living among the hills insures ; he had not thought of the quick sensitiveness which catches at an idea from a look, a movement, a chance glance.

However, Mr. Aggland was all the more presentable for the change in his attire, and as he proceeded to say, how he had thought the day might come when somebody in Norfolk would know he was Phemie's uncle, and that therefore —and to do such credit as he could to Captain Stondon—he wanted to make the best of himself, the officer was quite touched by the man's unselfish thoughtfulness, by the love and affection which had compelled him to make an exertion that a weaker nature would have been ashamed to confess.

Everything he saw about the farmer made him regret more and more that his life had proved so hard an one for himself, so profitless an one for others ; and this feeling made him treat his new friend in a manner which induced Mr. Aggland afterwards to declare to Phemie—

"If I had been a king, child, he could not have made more of me."

Nor was Mr. Aggland, who had seen some fine estates in his lifetime, less impressed with the stateliness of Marshlands than with the courtesy of its owner.

The house was "far and away grander than Worton Court," he told his niece, and if Mr. Aggland had entertained any doubts on the subject of Captain Stondon's social standing, his visit to Marshlands completely undeceived him.

He passed a week there—a whole week, though he had declared he "couldna, shouldna, daurna stay for more than a couple of days ;" and many a long talk had he and Captain Stondon, sitting over the library fire, whilst dessert remained untouched beside them, and each forgot to pass the decanter which contained some of that "inimitable '24 port."

It was great promotion for Phemie. The longer Mr. Aggland stayed at Marshlands, and the more he saw of the master of Marshlands, the more unreal the whole affair seemed; and he went meekly back to Cumberland, feeling that neither he nor his could ever have made the girl half so happy as it was in both the power and the will of this rich gentleman to do.

The marriage was to take place in the spring, and Captain Stondon wanted to provide Phemie's trousseau; but on this point Mr. Aggland was firm.

"There is no use in the child bringing her two or three halfpence in her hand to you," he said, not without a certain sadness; "and so we may just as well spend her little fortune on the only thing she is ever likely to have to provide for herself. She shall not disgrace any of us, I promise you that; and till she is your wife, I would rather she was not indebted to you for anything."

As usual, there was so much sense in what Mr. Aggland said, that Captain Stondon had to yield the point; and the consequence was that the farmer returned from London with such a quantity of luggage as caused his wife to stand aghast.

"Oh! Peggy; oh! Peggy," cried Phemie Keller. "Those boxes are like something out of fairyland: there are silks and laces, and muslins and ribbons, and the most enchanting kid shoes, and kid gloves, Peggy—French gloves, like Lady Wauthrope's. And whatever more I want, uncle says is to be ordered from Liverpool; but I shall never wear all those things out. I could not do it if I were to live for a thousand years. Come and look at them, and then tell me if you believe I am Phemie Keller. It is something like what we used to talk about, Peggy. Do you remember how we used to talk?"

"Ay, bairn, I mind it weel." The time Miss Phemie dreamed her dreams was not so very far remote but that any one could recollect it. "And it seems to me, when I'm thinking ower it a', that the Yerl has come across the hills to tak' my darling frae me."

"But you shall come too. I asked him about it, and he said, 'Yes, of course;' so you must get a trousseau, Peggy, and travel with us wherever we go."

"Ye dinna want an auld fule like me to wait on ye," answered Peggy; "an' if ye did, I'd rather stay i' the house I ken sae weel, wi' the maister who has been aye sae gude to me, than gang roamin' about the warld. But when ye are a great lady, mind I always said this would come to pass; for if he is not an yerl, he is as rich as one, I'll be bound."

"And I am sure he is kinder to me than any duke in the land could be," agreed Phemie; but Phemie sighed for all that—a deep sigh—for the vanished hopes, for the dream hero that could return to her no more!

CHAPTER XII.

FOR LIFE.

SPRING came to the sweet valley of Tordale—came with its flowers and sunshine—its showers—its springing grass—its budding trees—its balmy winds—its wealth of promise—across the hills and up the ravine.

By the dark green of the yarrow under foot—by the anemones and hyacinths blooming beneath the trees—by the soft cushions of lady's-fingers—by the scent of the clover in the meadows—by the ragged-robin trailing through the hedges—by the saxifrage growing beside the waterfall—by the ferns daintily unfolding their leaves—by the delicate colour of the moss covering the boulders—you could tell as you passed by that Spring had come, and was decking herself in robes of coolest verdure, to greet the richer beauty of the summer.

When the young lambs were dotted about on the mountain-sides—when marsh-marigolds and gowans were to be gathered in handfuls—when the streams and rills were dancing over the stones and making sweet melody as they sped along, thankful the winter snows were melted, the winter frosts thawed—Phemie Keller was married.

Ere ever the wild roses put forth buds—ere ever the honeysuckle climbing among thorn and briar and bramble began to scent the air with its delicious fragrance—in the spring-time of her young life—in the first bloom and blush of her rare loveliness—Phemie became a wife.

In the midst of the congregation, Captain Stondon met her a stranger—from the midst of the congregation he took her for himself.

Had he ever wanted to be rid of his bargain— to back out of the engagement entered into, where the Cumberland hills frowned down on Tordale Church—he would have found it no easy matter to do so, for the whole parish might have been summoned as witnesses on Phemie's behalf.

The shepherds left their sheep to the tender mercies of the coolies—the farmers put on their best suits and plodded up the valley to Tordale Church—the eggs were not collected—the milk was not churned—the children did not go to school on that fine spring morning when Phemie Keller was married.

Had privacy been desired, privacy would have been in Tordale simply impossible; and as no secret was made of the day or the hour, as everybody had known for weeks previously when the ceremony was to take place, the church was literally crammed.

Many a one who had never gone to hear Mr. Conbyr preach went to hear him read the words that made the bride and bridegroom one—went to see the grand gentleman, who was popularly supposed to have so much money that he did not know what to do with it, taking to wife Daniel Aggland's niece—bonnie Phemie, who, for all her great fortune, for all her fine clothes, looked pale and frightened, or, as one of the spectators remarked, "flate."

" There is a most serious deal of difference," he added, shaking his head solemnly; "she's but a bairn, with her glintin' hair, and her soft blue eyes, and her jimp waist that I could 'most span with my one hand. She's but a bairn, while he " —and the man took a long look at Captain Stondon, who was standing bare-headed, with the sunshine streaming full upon him—" Go'nows *how* old he is."

I should like to be able to sketch that interior for you, my reader. I should like to show you the men and the women and the children who filled the church, and looked with grave, interested faces at the group standing before the altar. I should like to paint for you the way the sunbeams fell on Phemie's hair, turning each thread to gold—how they showed her pale pure face to every soul in the church—how in her white dress she looked more lovely than ever.

The Agglands were there, all of them—all Phemie's relations, excepting the Kellers—all her friends—all her acquaintances—all who knew anything about her—were gathered together on that bright spring morning; but Captain Stondon had no one belonging to him present on the occasion. Even his best man was no fine gentleman from London, but merely a stray curate from Grassenfel, who could not have seemed more uncomfortable had he been going to be married himself.

Already Captain Stondon had found that the position of his wife's family in the social scale placed him in an awkward dilemma. There are always certain embarrassments entailed by differences of rank which are felt by Love the moment he walks out of doors with the lady of his choice.

The world cares for Mammon, though Cupid may not. Society is apt to make merry over the ways and manners of those who are not the *crême de la crême*, while the happy pair are absorbed in one another. The wedding at Tordale would have shocked the sensitive nerves of Captain Stondon's intimates; and, accordingly, prudently and sensibly he refrained from making himself a laughing-stock among his friends.

When we are at Rome we do as Rome does. When we are in the world we conform to its usages; and though Captain Stondon was marrying out of the world, he still meant to return to the world and take his bride thither with him.

The absence of all hypercritical guests was best for both Phemie and her uncle. They had admitted as much to one another; and yet the fact of none of the bridegroom's friends being present hurt them, and showed them clearly, as if the future had been spread out before their eyes, that from all old associations—from all old friends— from all old habits—Phemie Keller was passing swiftly away.

As the shadow fades from the hill-side, leaving no trace of where it has rested, so auburn hair and blue eyes was passing away from the old familiar life—from the rugged mountain scenery—from the drip of the waterfall—from the calm peacefulness—from the sweet monotony of that remote valley for ever.

She might come back again, but never the
Phemie she had been; never again might she look
out on life as she had done from the windows
of her dream castle ; she might never more gaze
upon the mountains with the same eyes; she
might never speak with the same thoughts and
wishes swelling in her heart.

She was going out to be another Phemie ; in
a different rank ; with different aims, and hopes,
and objects; with a difficult part to play; with a
difficult path to follow : no wonder that as the
farmers' wives saw the tears filling her eyes, and
rolling down her cheeks, they said, with an in-
tuitive, unreasoning pity, "God help her; and she
so young!"

So young ; that was the string everybody harped
on. It never seemed to have occurred to them
before, that she was barely more than a child, till
they came to see her pledging her whole future
—all the long, long years she had in all human
probability before her—away.

Many a one present had not liked Phemie over
much in days gone by. They had thought her

conceited, fanciful, stuck up ; but now that she was being made a lady of—now that the whole country side had been bidden to a marriage feast at the Hill Farm, and that the girl, in her sorrow and trouble at leaving everything behind her, had gone to bid even the veriest virago in Tordale good-bye—her short-comings were forgotten, and nothing but her youth and beauty remembered.

Her fine clothes, that she had been so proud to exhibit, were never thought of; the grand match she was making, and of which some present had been very jealous, faded out of recollection ; and for the time being her young face, her girlish figure, filled every heart with a vague pity. Something was wanting in that bridal group, and the spectators felt the want as they looked at the child giving herself to this man so long as he lived or as she lived.

There was not a person present—unless, indeed, it might be Mr. Aggland—who could have defined his or her sensations ; but, nevertheless, every one felt the absence of that intangible something which Phemie Keller might never now become acquainted with, sinlessly, through all the years to come.

That was it—for better, for worse—she was resigning all hope, all chance of happy love; love with its bliss and agony; love with its doubts and distractions; love without which no life, be it otherwise ever so symmetrical, can be perfect. Attachment—affection—a calm, even, unruffled existence is better, some tell you, than the hot and the cold, the fever and the collapse, the mad pulse and the shivering agony. It may be so. God knows what is best for us: God knew what was best for Phemie Keller!

And yet as the "keld" comes darkling upon the surface of the Cumberland lakes, without cloud, without wind, without shadow, without reason that we can trace, so in the middle of the sunshine, in the middle of the prosperity, a "keld" seemed to gather on the waters of Phemie's life; those clear waters that were as yet unruffled by passion, untroubled by regret.

For she was, as they all said, young. She was such a child that her composure was disturbed by Davie, who had thought it incumbent upon him to come and see the ceremony, like his neighbours.

A wise dog, he followed the wedding party from the Hill Farm at a distance, and had slunk into the church in an unassuming, undemonstrative manner, with his tail between his legs, doubtless hoping by this manœuvre to escape observation.

But Mrs. Aggland, ever lynx-eyed, spied him out, and bade Duncan take him home; an order which Duncan disputed in so loud a whisper that the controversy attracted the attention of one of the shepherds, who secured the dog, and placed him between his legs, from which position Davie surveyed the ceremony with sorrowful eyes.

When the company began to disperse, Davie walked out with the first, but waited, like a Christian, in the church porch for Phemic.

He knew as well as anybody there that she was going from him. Many a pleasant mile they had walked together over the hills; many a score times she had called him to follow her to Strammer Tarn; many a morning they had run down the hill-side and across the valley when the sun was looking at them over Helbeck in the glad summer, or in the dreary winter, when Phemie looked back gleefully to see her footprints in the snow. They had climbed together; they had rested among the heather; she had twined wild flowers round his neck, an attention he had not then appreciated; she had loved him and been good to him; and now it was all over, and Davie knew it, and because he knew it, he did not jump upon her, or fawn, or gambol, or bark as she came out.

He only wagged his dilapidated tail from side to side, and licked her hand, and looked up in her face, and said farewell as plainly as a dumb brute can.

At which performance Phemie—Phemie Keller no longer—broke out crying, to the dismay of Captain Stondon, who hurried her through the churchyard and down the steps, inwardly anathematizing Davie in particular, and the lookers on in general.

"It's all along of you," remarked Mrs. Aggland, giving Duncan a shake. "If you had taken the dog back, as I told you, she would have been all right. Was ever woman plagued as I am by a set of disobedient, headstrong boys ? "

" Well, you wouldn't have liked to go home yourself," retorted Duncan ; whilst Mr. Aggland, with a troubled look in his face, muttered as he walked along, leading Helen by the hand—

" An auld head set on shouthers young,
　The like was never seen ;
For bairnies will be bairnies aye,
　As they hae ever been."

But he was thinking of something else all the while. He was thinking about Phemie ; thinking, as he had never thought before, of the future she was going out to meet.

" Keep up, Phemie ; be brave," he found an opportunity of whispering to her, and the girl dried her tears, and smiled her best, and laughed when her husband broke the bridecake over her head, after the fashion of the country, while the young men and the young women contended for the very crumbs eagerly.

Then Captain Stondon was happy again. He

forgave Duncan and he forgave the inhabitants of Tordale, and he made himself so agreeable while Phemie was getting ready for her departure, that the bride's youth and the bride herself were forgotten, and everybody joined in praises of the officer, and wishes for his health, happiness, and prosperity.

The guests were going to keep up the feast till night, or at least so long as their heads remained tolerably steady, but the bride and bridegroom had to start early in the afternoon to catch the train at Carlisle, from which place Phemie had elected to go to Scotland to spend her honeymoon.

After that Captain Stondon proposed travelling, on the Continent, and the girl did not know when she should see her uncle or Cumberland again.

"I hope you will be happy, Phemie," he said; "I believe you will."

"I think I shall, uncle," she answered; but the tears were in her eyes as she spoke.

"I have something to say to you before you go," he began; "something that came into my mind as I followed you home from church."

"What is it?" she asked. "What is it?" she repeated, seeing that he paused and hesitated.

"If I was sending Duncan out into the world," he said, "I should warn him that it is a sinful world; that though it may not be hard to keep straight in a lonely place like this, it is not so easy to be good with temptations surrounding us on every side——"

"Yes, uncle," agreed Phemie.

"Burns says," proceeded Mr. Aggland, "that—

> ' Gentlemen an' ladies worst,
> Wi' ev'ndown want o' wark are curst.'

Now you are going to be a lady, Phemie, and a lady out in the world, and I do not want you to lose your head in consequence; I do not want you to live an objectless, useless, idle life. Chaucer tells us truly that—

> ' An ydil man is like an hous that hath nomne walls,
> The deviles may enter on every syde;'

and an idle woman's position is quite as bad, Phemie, quite."

"But I shall not be idle," she pleaded.

"You will not have to work," he answered,

"and that with many is synonymous with idleness. You are going to you know not what, my child," he went on; "you are going into a strange world, where there are strange fashions, strange creeds, strange ideas of morality. Phemie, you will keep yourself straight; you won't forget what I have tried to teach you; you won't forget what your grandfather taught you; you won't forget this world is not all, and that its fashions and its pleasures pass swiftly away?"

"I will try to be good, uncle."

"You will have servants under you," he continued. "Don't be hard with them, Phemie; don't be thoughtless. Remember they have souls to be saved as well as you. You have beauty. It is an article much prized where you are going. Don't be too vain of it. Remember God gave it to you—a gift not to be abused. Never forget that, unless allied to something better, it is but—

> ' A doubtful good, a gloss, a glass, a flower,
>   Lost, faded, broken, dead within an hour.'

You will be rich; when you are so, 'be not exalted,' as Cleobulus pithily puts it. Solomon says, 'riches are not for ever;' remember that; and also that for the use you make of them while you have them you will be held accountable. I would have you emulate those—

' Great souls, who touch'd with warmth divine,
   Give gold a price, and teach its beams to shine ;
   All hoarded pleasures they repute a load,
   Nor think their wealth their own, till well bestowed.'

But you are going into a world so new and strange that all old counsels, all old teachings, seem inapplicable to it."

And Mr. Aggland dropped his hand despairingly on Phemie's shoulder as he concluded.

"I will try to remember," she said.

"I would have you—

' Strive in youth
   To save your age from care,' "

continued her uncle. "I would have you keep every Christian grace, every womanly virtue. I do not wish to see you a fashionable lady. Do not at first be too confident, but proceed—

' Like one that on a lonesome road
   Doth walk in fear and dread.'

And yet I would not have you over-fearful, or

cowardly, because I know 'that what begins in fear usually ends in folly.' I want you to keep a balance, Phemie, between bigotry and irreligion— between virtue and prudery—between hard work and idleness—between confidence and presumption."

"I wish I had not to go away at all, uncle," was her comment on this string of advice.

"If you had not to go away I should not have to warn you," he answered. "And now good-bye, and don't forget me, Phemie; don't quite forget me, if you can help it."

He was parting from the girl he had loved like his own daughter; parting from her who was going forth on an untried, uncertain road; and if the tears did come into his eyes, if his voice did tremble for a moment, I hope those who read these pages will not think him the less a man for all that.

As for Phemie, seeing him in such trouble, she kept her own trouble back bravely. She would not cry; she would not unfit herself for saying what she knew was the truth, that she could

never forget him, nor forget the Hill Farm; and
she took his hand and kissed it ere he could prevent her, while she whispered—

> " The mother may forget the child
>   That smiles sae sweetly on her knee,
> But I'll remember thee, Glencairn,
>   And a' that thou hast done for me."

And then she broke down—then she threw herself into his arms and lay sobbing there till
Helen came to remind her time was getting on,
and that railway trains wait for no one.

"You must go now, Phemie," said her uncle;
"do not think me unkind for hurrying you
away—

> ' I have too grieved a heart to take a tedious leave.'

There now. Let's not unnerve each other," and
he put her gently back from him. "And now
for my last words. Remember that you are
but an—

> ' Unlessoned girl, unschooled, unpractised.
>   Happy in this—you are not yet so old
>   But you may learn.'

Be a good wife to the man who has chosen you,

and whom you have chosen. 'Do him good, and not evil, all the days of your life.' Now, Phemie, now—now," and he unclasped the arms she had thrown round him once again, and bade her say what other farewells she had to say, as it was high time they were off to Carlisle.

"I shall come back again," Phemie said to each and all. "I shall come back again, Duncan. I will indeed, Helen. Be sure I won't stay long away, Peggy."

But Peggy M'Nab refused to be comforted. She went into her kitchen after the happy pair drove away, and covered her head with her apron, and sobbed aloud.

"Don't cry, Peggy!—don't, don't!" exclaimed Helen, with the tears streaming down her own cheeks; "don't cry; she will come back to us; you heard her say yourself that she would."

"Alake, Miss Helen," answered Peggy, from behind her curtain of blue check, "the child that I carried in my airms—that I nursed in my lap— I have not seen this mony a year, unless, maybe, by an odd time in a dream; and your cousin

Phemie, who has just gane awa', neither you nor me will ever set eyes on again till our deein' day."

At which assurance Helen lifted up her voice and wept aloud, for she did not understand the exact meaning of the hard truth contained in Peggy's pathetic words. And if she had, would she have wept the less? Would she have ceased lamenting? Would it have been any consolation to her to know that another Phemie might come back, but that the Phemie who had danced over the heather, and sat by Strammer Tarn, and assisted in all household duties; who had been gay and sad, happy and sorrowful, could return to the Hill Farm—to the peace and quiet of the valley below—to the rugged mountains—to the murmuring waterfall—never more—ah, never!

CHAPTER XIII.

DISAPPOINTED.

MONTAGUE STONDON, Esquire, barrister-at-law, heir presumptive to Marshlands, fifteenth, or twentieth, or thirtieth cousin, or something equally near of kin to the man who had just taken unto himself a wife, lived in Chapel Street, Grosvenor Place, in a house which commanded in front a cheerful view of the other side of the way, and at the back looked out over Tattersall's to St. George's Hospital.

It was not a large house, it was not a convenient one, it was far and away too expensive for Mr. Stondon's means; but it was sufficiently genteel, it was within five minutes of the Row, it was close to the Green Park, it touched elbows with Belgrave Square, and altogether suited the barrister as well as any house is ever likely to suit any man who is overwhelmed with debt, and who, having the tastes of a millionaire, is often at his wits' end to know where to raise twenty pounds.

If you are not bidden to a banquet, I cannot see the precise pleasure that accrues from beholding others partaking of it. If you have not the means to visit with his Grace the Duke, it is beyond my capacity to understand why you should pay fabulous rents for the mere enjoyment of living near his Grace, and seeing her Grace's carriage pass your door; but Montague Stondon felt that there was a satisfaction in residing within call of nobility, and that their footmen, their equipages, their crests, and coats of arms conferred a certain importance on him. The earth would not be a very cheerful dwelling-place if it were beyond reach of the sun's rays, and in the opinion of Montague Stondon the sun never rose except about Belgrave Square and those other regions affected by the nobility and gentry of England.

When he rode out on his hired horse, he could be in the midst of rank and fashion immediately;

he could take his fine whiskers into the Park and air them there, while he gnawed the handle of his riding-whip, and wondered how the deuce he was to carry on for a year or two longer.

When Mrs. Stondon, a faded fashionable woman, who had brought her husband some fortune, " received," she liked to think that the carriages of her visitors and the carriages of the great people hard by touched wheels in the street.

It was nice to lie on the sofa and listen to the thundering double knocks powdered footmen were giving in the neighbouring square; it would have been impossible to have ordered goods home, if home had chanced to be outside the radius of fashion; it would have done Basil harm at school had his parents not lived in a genteel quarter; it would have been fatal to him at college had the parental letters been dated from any locality less desirable than Chapel Street.

Fashion—even the flimsiest and falsest kind of fashion—was a good to be purchased at any price, at any risk. They had been used to it—they had been accustomed to terrible dinner parties, to r owded assemblies, to boxes at the Opera, to all the hundred weary pleasures which so many Londoners consider necessary to their very existence; and the consequence was that, as they could not relinquish any of their usual indulgences, they got more and more involved while the years went by, and less and less able to extricate themselves from their embarrassments.

But for the hope of Marshlands, but for the idea that some day they should have money in plenty, life would scarcely have been supportable. As it was, they went on their way, trusting that news would soon come of Captain Stondon's death, and of their own accession to fortune.

" What right has a man like that to own such a property ? " demanded Mrs. Montague Stondon. "He might just as well give it to us for all the enjoyment he takes out of it. I am positive he cannot spend more than five hundred a year !" and the lady sighed at the idea of Marshlands belonging to a person who could so limit his personal expenditure.

As for his profession, Montague Stondon made

very little of it. If he possessed any natural abilities he never used them. If there was money to be earned at the Bar, scarcely any of it found its way into his pocket. He was good company, but he was not much of an opinion. He could shoot better than he could plead; he liked lounging in his own drawing-room, cantering up the Row, criticising the latest beauty, far more than sütting in his chambers or cross-examining witnesses.

His manners would have brought him business, his address made him a favourite with the judges; but his intense dislike for work, his inordinate love of pleasure, rendered his career a failure, his whole existence but a race after amusement, a longing for dead men's shoes, a staving-off of duns, an incessant struggle with debt and poverty.

It is astonishing how miserably poor, people living in a respectable manner, inhabiting a house in a desirable neighbourhood, keeping several servants, eating of the best, sleeping on the softest, may really be. The sempstress living in Bethnal

Green had not more anxiety for the morrow, more care for the day, than Montague Stondon, Esq., of Chapel Street, Grosvenor Place, who was over head and ears in debt, and who spent that portion of his life which he passed in the bosom of his family in alternately cursing his luck and praying for the death of his relative.

"If that fellow do not soon go home," he remarked one morning to his wife, "I shall have to figure in the 'Gazette;' we cannot carry on much longer as we are doing now!" and he flung down letter after letter containing requests for debts recently incurred, more pressing demands for bills of longer standing, and threats of law from creditors whose large stock of patience was at last fairly exhausted. "I am sure I do not know what we are to do unless we can retrench."

"Retrench!" repeated Mrs. Stondon, raising her light eyebrows at the very idea. "How are we to do that? If you can show me how it is possible for us to retrench," she proceeded, with quite a show of energy, "I am willing to begin." And the lady went on opening her letters, while

Montague Stondon took refuge behind the "Times," muttering, as he did so,

"Willing or not, there will soon have to be something done, I see that plainly."

Meantime Mrs. Stondon read her letters. They were, as a rule, the customary letters which ladies write to ladies, crossed as if note-paper had been ten guineas a quire and postage three shillings the half ounce; but occasionally there intervened a short curt note from some indignant milliner, or a pathetic entreaty for money from a struggling dressmaker.

These Mrs. Stondon dropped as though they had burnt her fingers; but to the small gossip, the petty tittle-tattle, the long rambling epistles of her friendly correspondents, she devoted herself with praiseworthy earnestness.

"Mary Monk is going to be married,"—these were the pieces of information to which she treated her husband—"a very nice match, Mrs. Monk says. Three thousand a year, and a most lovely place in Derbyshire. So devotedly attached to her, and so fond of all her family. Well, Mrs.

Monk is fortunate—she has got rid of four out of the seven now. Julia Enon has another boy, so there will be no want of heirs there; and Sir John Martingale has proposed for and been accepted by a widow who has a hundred thousand pounds fortune. Caroline wants us to go and stay with her for a month before she leaves for the Continent, and Mrs. Leigh hopes we will not forget them this summer. What a pleasant world this would be if one had plenty of money!" sighed Mrs. Stondon, laying down Mrs. Leigh's letter and taking up another.

"I wonder who this is from?" she said, turning it over; "post-mark Grassenfel—who do we know in Grassenfel, Montague?"

"That is the place where Henry was laid-up at," answered her husband, his interest excited in a moment. "I wish to heaven he had broken his neck there!"

"Hush! you should not say such things," expostulated his wife.

"Only think them, I suppose," was his reply. "Well, what have you got? What have you got,

I say ?" and he snatched the enclosure out of his wife's hand, and read—

"CAPTAIN STONDON,—MRS. STONDON."

"Damn him!" said Mr. Montague Stondon, when he had taken in what it all meant. "Damn her—damn them both!"

And having concluded this little commination service, he looked at his wife, and his wife looked at him; and then they looked with one accord at the bills and letters strewing the breakfast-table.

"It is a cursed shame!" broke out Mr. Stondon, and his brown eyes seemed to grow black with rage as he spoke; "a man ought to be locked up for doing such a thing—at his time of life, too! He must be mad—he has no right to be at large!"

"Some designing creature, doubtless," wept Mrs. Stondon.

"That cuts Basil out for ever," said Mr. Stondon, with another oath.

"She may not have any children," observed

his wife, clutching at the only straw within reach.

"Won't she?" answered the barrister, "won't she? by George! She'll have scores of them, and Basil may go and enlist as soon as he likes, for none of us will ever touch a penny of the Marshlands rents now."

"I wonder who she is, Montague? Look in the 'Times' and see if it is there."

And it was there.

"At Tordale, by the Rev. Edward Conbyr, Vicar—Henry Gower Stondon, Esq., late Captain in the —th Hussars, to Euphemia, only daughter of the late Ernest Keller, Esq., and niece of General Keller, Roundwood, Sussex."

"How the deuce did he meet one of the Roundwood Kellers at Grassenfel?" demanded Mr. Stondon, and his wife said feebly that she really did not know.

"Depend upon it," went on the barrister, "there is something queer about the business, otherwise he never would have kept it so quiet. There is a screw loose somewhere, but that won't

do us any good. He might just as well have
broken his neck." And Montague Stondon, aged
a dozen years in as many minutes, tossed over his
bills with the air of a man who did not know
which way to turn for assistance. "It will bring
them all down upon me," he said; and he began
swearing once again, when his wife suggested that
perhaps Captain Stondon would help him over his
difficulties and do something for Basil.

"You do not know what you are talking
about," was his reply; "you do not know how
much we owe. It would not take a shilling less
than ten thousand pounds to put us straight, and
you do not expect him to give us that, I suppose,
with a wife in the present, and a tribe of children
coming?."

"She may not have any family," repeated Mrs.
Stondon.

"I tell you she will," answered her husband.
"Women always have children when you don't
want them to have any; and even if she have
not, what good will that be to us? She will take
care of him now, and he will live for—God only

knows how long." And Mr. Montague Stondon thrust the ends of his whiskers into his mouth, and chewed them savagely, while he wrought out this problem to his own dissatisfaction.

For a minute some vague idea of setting to work even at the eleventh hour—of struggling for wealth, position, ease—crossed the barrister's mind.

What was the good of such a life, after all ? Where was the pleasure of running into debt ? What did the opinion of the world signify? What did it matter whether he met fifty fashionable people in the course of the day, who were as perfectly indifferent to him as he was to them ? Was this weary game worth the price of the candle which he was burning down and down, day after day, and week after week ? Could he do nothing to retrieve the past ? or was it too late for everything but debt, and duns, and discontent ?

"If he had any family pride, I would go into trade to spite him," said the barrister at last. "I would take a shop and put on an apron, and paint Montague Stondon, grocer, up in the High Street of Disley, as fast as I would walk into the Park; but he would only say he hoped I should do a good business, and offer to pay my rent for the first year, and tell me to send over half a dozen pounds of tea to Marshlands. Hang him!" finished Mr. Stondon, with fervour. "I wish he was being tried for his life at the Old Bailey, and that I was for the Crown. He should die if he had fifty lives; he should swing from a gallows as high as Haman's, if I had any voice in the matter."

"My dear Montague!" entreated Mrs. Stondon.

"He might just as well and better have died in India," proceeded her husband; "nobody would have missed him, and I should then have succeeded to Marshlands. When a man goes out to India, he is expected to stay there, and he has no right to come back to stand in the way of his relations. I wish I was twenty years younger, I would show Captain Stondon how a man may get on without Marshlands: but Basil shall work.

He shall not lead the life I have done. If I could but get rid of these cursed liabilities, I would think about him."

"Perhaps Captain Stondon would do something," suggested the lady.

"He only paid for his education when he was single," retorted the barrister; "do you think he will do more now he is married?" And Mrs. Stondon had to take refuge in her private opinion, which was that the very first time she had a chance she would "humble herself," as she expressed it, to her kinsman, and ask him to help Mr. Stondon, and to push on her son.

"Only give me an opportunity," thought this wise lady, "and I will improve it."

And without saying a word to her husband, the very day she heard of Captain Stondon's arrival in town, she called upon the bride, whom she offered to take with her to every possible and impossible place; whom she kissed; whom she flattered; whom she treated as though Phemie had been one of the blood royal, or a countess in her own right.

Then she told Mr. Stondon that he must call also, and Mr. Stondon called.

"The girl is pretty," he said, on his return home, "and I do not think she has fooled him. It is her face that has done it; and somehow or other, though how I can't imagine, it is a great match for her. She has no manners; she has no confidence; she is just an unfledged country wench whom he has fallen in love with on account of her beauty;" and Montague Stondon cursed her beauty, and wished all women were born a hundred years old and as ugly as witches. "She will lead him a pretty dance before long," finished the barrister; "why there must be forty years between them: he might be her grandfather. Do you know how they happened to meet with one another, and who made her marry him? for, of course, she never did it of her own free will."

"I know nothing," answered Mrs. Montague Stondon. "I have never seen her alone; he will not trust her out of his sight. I said if he had any business to attend to, before he went abroad, I would try to amuse her; but he said that he had no business, and that he thought 'Phemie,' as he calls her, would like best to go about with him. And if you believe me, Montague," went on the lady, "the girl said she did not want to go anywhere without him; an ungrateful minx! and I think she is fond of him; positively, my dear, I think she is."

"So should I be, if he gave me Marshlands," answered Mr. Stondon.

"Ah! but I mean without Marshlands. I think she is one of those soft, pulpy, characterless girls who like anybody who is fond of them. Whatever he says, she agrees with. She does nothing but blush and answer every question through him. 'I do not know what Captain Stondon intends to do.' 'Henry, where shall we be going to first?' 'Shall we return to England this year, Henry?' It is Henry this, and Henry that, and 'May I, Henry?'—perfectly disgusting, you know; bad enough when the husband is a boy, but simply ridiculous when he might be her great-grandfather."

"I must try to get something more out of her

when they dine here," remarked Mr. Stondon;
" you have asked them, have you not ? "

"Yes," answered Mrs. Stondon, "and what is
more, they are coming.   I thought I never should
have persuaded Captain Stondon, but he ulti-
mately yielded.   I suppose the bride knows
nothing of *les convenances*, and that he is afraid
of her making some *faux pas.*"

" Poor little soul ! " ejaculated the barrister.

"Little simpleton," remarked his wife.

CHAPTER XIV.

ON VIEW.

WHEN Mrs. Montague Stondon invited her relations to dine with them in "a quiet way," she assured Captain Stondon that she would not ask more than a couple, or so, of friends to meet them.

"It will be only a family party," she declared, and then forthwith she wrote notes to about five-and-twenty people, of whom the one-half had pleasure in accepting.

"I could not get through the dinner with that pair alone," she informed her husband; "and if we have one or two, we may as well have a dozen. It is no more trouble, and it is no more expense; and although Captain Stondon talks so much about not caring for society, I know he would not like to spend an evening *téte-à-téte* with us. That is the way with all those kind of men. They do not know what they want! If the bride acquits herself creditably he will be as proud as a peacock, and it shall not be my fault if she do not."

"Nor mine," added Mr. Stondon, for all which kind intentions Phemie would have been duly grateful had she only known of them.

As it was, she dreaded that visit as she had never dreaded anything before in her life, and the hints and instructions which Captain Stondon thought it necessary to give only made her original confusion worse. He told her she must not do this, and that she must do something else. He fidgeted about her dress; he would not let her maid arrange her hair, but sent for an individual with elaborate whiskers, who made her head ache, and sent her out unable to bend her neck.

"I do not think going to Court could be much worse than this!" sighed Phemie, as she fitted on her gloves; but she felt comforted when her husband surveyed her proudly, and told her she was the prettiest creature he had ever seen.

"Am I really pretty, Henry?" asked the girl, who had begun to question her own good looks, and to value her personal possessions at a much more modest rate than formerly.

"Are you really what?" he retorted, holding her at arm's length from him, and proudly surveying her from head to foot. "Are you really what?—oh, vanity! vanity!" and then Phemie laughed and blushed to hear again and again that she was beautiful.

But no consciousness of beauty could have made that dinner-party other than a wretched ordeal to the young wife. The faces of twelve strangers whom she had never seen previously, swam before her. Thirty eyes were always, as she imagined, riveted on her. If Mr. Stondon would only have let her alone; if he had only not tried to make her talk; if the servants could only have believed that she was not famishing, and that she did not want a glass of wine every other minute; if the light had not been so strong;

if the room had not been so close ; if everything
had been different, Phemie thought she could
have managed better : as it was, she envied Mrs.
Stondon, she envied the servants, she envied
every person and any person who knew what was
what, and she envied, beyond all other persons, a
young lady who, owing to there being seven on a
side, sat next to her, and whose composure filled
Phemie with the most intense admiration, not to
say awe.

If she had upset her wine, if she had spilled
her soup, if she had taken mint sauce with duck,
if she had kept the whole table waiting, if she had
answered without being spoken to, if she had
dropped her fork, if she had appropriated her
neighbour's bread, that wonderful woman would
have shown no more sign of embarrassment than
if she had done everything decently and in
order.

Talking to a gentleman on her right hand, she
let a morsel of chicken fall from her fork, and the
misadventure made Phemie feel as though she
had committed some sin herself.

"That was a great disappointment," remarked the culprit to her, with a charming smile, and then straightway she observed to her other neighbour, "which shows people should not try to do two things at once."

"If I could learn to be like her," thought Phemie, jealously, "I should not mind paying a thousand pounds, supposing I had the money."

Have patience, child, have patience—Rome was not built in a day. If the gift be so valuable, rest content, for it will come to you yet; if ease of manner and indifference to the opinions of others be possessions worth coveting, rest satisfied, for in the years now before you all diffidence will vanish and fade away, and you shall care no more for speaking to a countess than you ever did to a farmer's wife in Tordale.

But be not over eager, *ma mignonne*, for the human being has yet to be created who shall retain a child's heart under a woman's manner. Is it worth the price, Phemie? Is the external ease and grace and self-possession a fair exchange for the internal suffering and loss that must first be incurred? In this world do we get anything cheaply? On this side heaven can we secure any prize without paying dearly for it? It is better to be embarrassed at a dinner-party than to sit nursing care o'nights. It is better that society should have our worst than that we should be miserable when the guests are gone and the doors closed. The day may come when you will look back to the blushing, timid, ignorant Phemie, three parts through her teens, and wish you could steal her back from the past to have and to hold for ever—wish unavailingly, for along the road you will then have travelled there is no return, and the Phemie you can dimly remember—the Phemie who was married while yet almost a child in Tordale Church, may return to you in the flesh, only when the rivers flow back to their springs, when the grain ripens in December, and the flowers and the trees bloom and look green among winter frosts and snows.

Nevertheless Phemie envied her companion, and wished with all her heart that the calumet of peace she and the Captain had come to smoke in

Chapel Street had not assumed the form of a dinner-party.

How could she guess that care was sitting beside her hostess likewise?—how could she imagine, looking at the plate, the glass, the china, the servants, the wines, the fruits, that Mrs. Stondon had not found it easy to arrange her materials? that there was a terrible to-morrow, and a more terrible morrow after, coming to the smiling woman at the head of the table? How could she foresee the end which came to Montague Stondon, to his debts, to his embarrassments, to his dinners, to his hopes, to his schemes? When he took her under his especial protection later on in the evening, and began "drawing her out," she, looking at his fine figure, at his handsome face, never realised how stiff and stark would be the one, how fixed and ghastly the other, ere she set foot in England again.

If she could have turned over a few pages and read to the point where "the end" was written across his life, she would have been tolerant and sorrowful; as it was, she saw merely his brown eyes searching her through, she heard only his soft voice asking her questions, which were full of torture to her.

"She liked flowers, he was certain;" so he took her to see the conservatory, which was always full of bloom, let who would, go without money. "You must not compare our plants with those you are accustomed to at Roundwood," he went on; "General Keller's gardens are famous all over Sussex, I am told."

Phemie kept silence for a moment. She did not know whether Captain Stondon would like her to say she and the Kellers were far apart as the poles; and, on the other hand, she felt it would not be truthful for her to let Mr. Stondon think she had ever seen her father's birthplace.

She had not lived all the most impressionable part of her life, however, with Mr. Aggland for nothing, and accordingly she answered timidly, though with the tell-tale colour that offended Mrs. Stondon flushing her face—

"I think your flowers beautiful, and I have never been at Roundwood."

"Then you have a pleasure more to come," replied Mr. Stondon. "I suppose it is stale news to you that your aunt is in town. I saw her in the Park yesterday."

Phemie's thoughts flew back to the cruel letter with which her aunt had severed all ties between them ; and forgetting everything except that and the contemptuous repulse her mother had received from the Keller family, she retorted hotly—

"That she did not know anything about Miss Keller, and did not want to know. She had never seen her, and she hoped she never should see her ; " after which statement, feeling she had committed herself, the girl grew scarlet, and stooping down over the flowers, commenced admiring them insanely.

"What does your mamma say to the idea of your staying away from her for so long a time ? " asked Mr. Stondon, smiling. She was such a foolish little fish, and he was so skilful an angler (this was what he thought), that there was no use in wasting valuable bait upon her.

"I have not any mamma," replied Phemie.

"She has been dead ever since I can remember, I was going to say; but I can remember her, so that would not be true. She has been dead ever so many years—ever so many;" and the bride bent her head again, and Montague Stondon knew it was to hide the tears that were brimming in her eyes.

He was beginning to like her. If she had been anybody else than his relation's wife, he would have commenced a flirtation. She had divine hair, she had sweet eyes, she had a delicious voice, with the faintest, slightest Northern accent to make it earnest and pathetic. She was soft and pulpy, as Mrs. Montague Stondon said; but then men are not usually averse to even an exaggeration of feminine perfections.

She was astonishingly pretty, and young, and impulsive. The kind of girl it was possible to fancy kissing a man out of gratitude if he had done her a great service; a charming girl, with the tenderest expression, with the whitest skin, with the frankest manner, with the most extraordinary want of self-confidence.

"I do not blame him," thought Montague Stondon; "though she may have a dozen brats, and I lose Marshlands, I do not blame him."

"I did not mean to pain you," he said gently. "I knew you had lost your father, but I did not think you had lost your mother too; forgive me." And he looked so penitent that Phemie could not choose but say—

"I have nothing to forgive, only it always makes me sorry to talk about my mother. She was so pretty, and she died so young."

Phemie was pretty too; would she die young? Mr. Stondon, looking into her face, would have helped that selfish question presenting itself if he could; but if Phemie was nice, Marshlands was nicer; and though he did not blame Captain Stondon for marrying her, it was impossible for him to avoid speculating on what might yet be if she were to die.

"It would kill him," considered the barrister. "How mercenary poverty makes a man! how good people who have plenty of money ought to be!" And then he said out loud, with a smile, "that he felt certain she had found some one to take her mother's place."

"I have always found more fathers than mothers," answered Phemie; and for all he tried hard to avoid laughing, Mr. Stondon was obliged to do so outright, while Phemie, her little hand resting on his arm, stood wondering what she could have said to amuse him, wondering if she had made any mistake—done anything wrong.

"My grandfather took care of me first," she explained, "and then my uncle, and—don't you think Captain Stondon may be wondering where I am, and wanting me?" added Phemie, conscious she was getting into deep water, and feebly struggling back to land.

"You mean your grandfather, Mr. Keller," suggested Mr. Stondon, as he led her towards the drawing-room.

"No," answered Phemie, impatiently. "If the Kellers had brought me up, I should have seen Roundwood; but I had nothing to do with them; I lived with my mother's father, a clergyman, till he died, and after that with my uncle in Cumberland."

"Is he a clergyman, too?" demanded her host.

"No—he is—he is—" and Phemie, knowing that Mr. Stondon's eyes were fixed upon her, grew first hot and then cold, and then angry with herself for fearing to say out openly in that genteel London house how her honest uncle got his living honestly.

With a bitter pang of shame she remembered his kindness, and contrasted it with her cowardice. In a moment it swept through her mind that it was like disowning him not to stand up and do battle, if need were, for the man who had been as a father to her.

"He is a farmer," she finished, with a defiant uplifting of her beautiful head. "He is a farmer;" and the evening light fell softly on her face as she spoke.

The same light was lying across Tordale then; the shadows were creeping up Helbeck; they were darkling down on the valley. Almost unconsciously Phemie, as she saw the expression which came over Mr. Stondon's face, turned and looked back at Tordale with the eyes of her heart, and as she looked she wished she was standing beside the waterfall, or among the flowers in her uncle's little garden, that she knew were giving out their fullest sweetness in that quiet evening hour.

"Shall we have to stay here long?" she asked her husband when she could escape from Mr. Stondon, and get over to the other side of the room. "I am *so* tired."

And she looked so tired that Captain Stondon observed, pityingly, "Poor child!" before he proceeded to say that Mrs. Stondon was most anxious to hear her sing. "You must make allowances for her," he added, turning to that lady; "she has lived all her life in the country, and been unable to receive proper instruction."

Whereupon Mrs. Montague Stondon declared she was quite certain she should be charmed; and, indeed, to do her justice, she had made up her mind to go into ecstacies if Phemie only screamed like a ballad-singer in the street.

Had not Captain Stondon promised to take care Basil was not disappointed in his long-talked-of trip to Norway, and did not she feel certain he would give her husband a few hundreds to stay the wolves for a time, at any rate?

Altogether, Mrs. Montague Stondon had done her work better than the barrister. If she could have imagined the mess he had got into with Phemie, she would have shaken him, weak and languid though she professed to be. Had she known how thoroughly the bride disliked him, how perfectly she understood Mr. Stondon thought her a "thing in the way," she would scarcely have addressed herself so amiably to her guest.

"What style of music do you prefer? Did you bring any of your songs with you? No! well, perhaps some of mine will suit your voice." And Mrs. Stondon began turning over the pieces that lay on the piano.

"What, none of them?" exclaimed the barrister's wife in despair. "What, none of them? Can you not recollect anything? Not one tiny ballad?"

and Mrs. Montague Stondon grew quite pathetic about the matter.

"The difficulty is that Phemie does not accompany herself," said Captain Stondon at this juncture.

"Perhaps," suggested the lady who had excited Phemie's envy at dinner, "perhaps I can smooth away that difficulty, if Mrs. Stondon will only tell me what she would like best to sing;" and she pulled off her gloves, and spread out her skirts, and sat down to the piano, and ran over the notes, triumphantly glancing up at poor, fluttering, confused Phemie the while, with a look which said—"Why are you not as I am? There is nothing to frighten you."

"What shall it be?" she asked, playing with chords and scales and chromatic passages carelessly as she spoke. "Some one mentioned ballads. Was it Scotch ballads—'Jock o' Hazeldean,' for instance?" and she just swept Phemie's face with her dark eyes ere she bent them on some music Captain Stondon placed before her.

"I know that," the bride remarked in a low voice.

"'You'll remember me,'" answered the lady. "Sing it then by all means." And thus commanded, Phemie began.

But she never ended. She broke down hopelessly, ignominiously. She got frightened ; she got confused. The strange room, the strange faces, the unaccustomed accompaniment, the novelty of her position, the very sound of her own voice alarmed her. She did her best ; she fought against her embarrassment ; she struggled on ; she sang a false note ; she made a desperate effort to recover herself; then she wavered and went wrong past redemption.

"It was all my fault," remarked her accompanist, cheerfully ; "try the last verse."

"I cannot, I cannot, indeed," said Phemie, almost crying, not daring to look round, mortified, angry, and ashamed. "I shall never try to sing again. I cannot sing before any one. I shall never try."

"Oh yes, you will," laughed her new friend.

" You will go abroad ; you will have lessons ; you
will gain courage ; you will cease to be diffident ;
you will learn to be confident ; and finally, you
will return to England, and sing 'Then you'll
remember' to me as often as I like to ask you.
Seriously, you have a splendid voice, and if it
were not breaking a commandment I should
covet it."

Looking at the speaker, Phemie straightway
did break the commandment, and envied her :
envied her beauty, her figure, her ease, and
grace.

What curls she had !—what a magnificent
neck !—what a lovely dress !—what a way of
putting things !

She was like a picture out of one of Heath's
" Books of Beauty."　She was like a heroine of romance—with her long lashes—with her round arms
—with her flowing hair—with her smile half gay,
half pensive. Everything Phemie had ever dreamed
of as most lovely in her sex was there for her to
fall down before and worship, if she would ; but
instead of worshipping she envied—silly child—

a woman who was not half so charming as herself. Is not auburn hair as beautiful as raven curls ?—have not men sighed for a glance from blue eyes as well as from black ?—has not seventeen its attractions—its young spring freshness—its soft loveliness—though it cannot possess the easy grace, the finished manner of five-and-twenty ? And did not five-and-twenty, with all her social advantages, look with a kind of speculative interest—with a vague regret at seventeen, who thought breaking down in a song the most terrible misfortune that could happen to her, and who wanted to get away and cry over her mishap.

If she could only ever hope to acquire a tenth portion of Miss Derno's self-possession she would be satisfied. If she could only talk as she talked—answer questions without a change of colour—play whatever she was requested to play—Phemie thought she should have nothing more to ask from heaven. And she sat and considered these things in the corner of a distant sofa where Mrs. Montague Stoudon had placed her, while that lady looked her new relative over as she might have done a piece of handsome silk in a draper's shop.

All at once Phemie came back from her musings, or, rather, having followed them out to a definite point, she looked up abruptly, and said,

" Can you tell me how old Miss Derno is ? "

Now there was a question to be put suddenly to a well-bred hostess !—and by a girl, too, whom she had decided did not possess a second idea.

" Why do you ask ? " inquired Mrs. Montague Stondon, with one of her sweetest smiles.

" Because I want to know," answered Phemie, simply.

" How very singular ! " exclaimed her hostess ; "how very odd!   How deliciously straightforward you are !   Miss Derno cannot be more than five-and-twenty, though she looks nearly thirty. Now, will you tell me why you wanted to know ? "

" Only that I might see how many years older she is than I," replied Phemie.

" A great many, I imagine," laughed Mrs. Stondon.

"She is half my lifetime older," said the girl, earnestly.

"I dare say she is ; but what then ?"

"Why, only that one may do ever so much in half a lifetime."

"I know some one who might do anything she chose," answered Mrs. Montague Stondon, and Phemie coloured to the very roots of her hair at having her own thoughts put into such exceedingly plain English.

"Eight years!—what might she not do in eight years? That was what she began pondering and considering. She could learn—she could gain knowledge—she could work hard—she could acquire such information as might make the man who had married her, proud of her instead of ashamed.

For Phemie felt confident he must be ashamed of her. It might have been all very well at Tordale, but in London, and amongst all these grand people (as the girl in her innocence considered them), he must be ashamed of the wife he had chosen.

She felt her heart beat faster and the blood rush up into her face as she recalled a glance that she had seen exchanged between a pair of ladies when she broke down in her song so hopelessly. A raising of the eyebrows, a mere curl of the lips, the slightest shrug of the shoulders, told Phemie their thoughts as clearly as though they had spoken them outright.

And it was so hard—so hard because she knew she had a better voice than Miss Derno—and singing was her sole accomplishment, and Captain Stondon had been proud of it! He would never ask her to sing again; he would be afraid. He would——

"So you really are going to leave London in two days," said Miss Derno at this juncture, breaking in suddenly on her reverie. "How I envy you! How I wish I was going through Switzerland, and to Rome, and to Naples, instead of down to a lonely country house on the borders of civilization, where we get letters about once a week, and see a stranger only when a vessel is wrecked on the coast!"

"I lived in a place as quiet as that," answered Phemie, "and liked it."

"Possibly; but you will like it no more. You could never go back and like it again. Solitude may be very charming, but society is more charming still. The world may be very hollow, but it is made up of our fellow-creatures for all that; and we cannot live without our fellow-creatures, bad as they are, for the simple reason that we are gregarious animals, and that angelic company is not obtainable on earth. Added to which," finished Miss Derno, "I think angels would be a little dull."

"I wish," said Phemie, "you were going abroad too. I should like it so much."

"So should I," answered Miss Derno, "but duty calls me to the ends of the earth, and I obey the summons. When you are in Paris, Vienna, or in any one of the hundred towns Captain Stondon says he intends taking you to see, think of me killing time—or, rather, being killed by time—in a place fifteen miles from everything—from letters—from papers—from books—from a doctor—from a station. There is no necessary of life near us excepting the churchyard, and we have no society, unless a curate who wears thick boots and spectacles, and his lame wife and about twenty-seven children, can be called desirable neighbours."

"What do you do all day?" asked her auditor.

"We sleep a great deal, and we eat every hour or so, and we watch the vessels passing, through a telescope; and we wonder where they are going. Then we drive; and I ride, and walk; and some one or other of the curate's children is always getting maimed; and when the doctor has happily to be sent for, he calls at the great house, and brings us news of the outer world—of the latest suicide, of the most interesting murder. But there is my aunt preparing for departure. I must say good-bye. *Au revoir.*"

"I am afraid it will not be *au revoir*," said Phemie. "We are to be away for so long a time that it is not likely we shall see each other again ever."

Miss Derno laughed. "There is no 'for ever'

in society. Everybody meets every one sooner or later ; and, recollect, when we do meet you are to sing 'You'll remember' without a mistake. If we were to be parted for twenty years the first thing I should say to you would be, 'That song, Mrs. Stondon.' So do not forget."

And she pressed Phemie's hand in hers, and was gone before the girl could answer.

CHAPTER XV.

FIVE years after Mrs. Montague Stondon's little party in Chapel Street, the 3·55 express was tearing along the Eastern Counties line to Disley under the glare of the afternoon sun.

"It was the hottest day that summer," so every passenger said, and so every passenger had abundant reason for thinking. The dust was intolerable—the heat unendurable; if you kept the windows down you were choked, blinded, and generally driven distracted with dust, grit, smoke, and small gravel; if you pulled the windows up, you had dust still, and were roasted, baked and boiled into the bargain.

When passengers got in, at the few stations where the train paused for such refreshment as could be afforded to it by water for its boiler, and oil for its wheels, each man and each woman seemed to bring a fire with him or her into the carriage. If they had been furnaces, instead of flesh and blood, they could not have added more to the discomfort of their neighbours than was the case.

The soda-water and sherry, the lemonade, the ginger-beer, which suffering humanity demanded at Cambridge as an alleviation of its miseries, might have been poured from a boiling kettle, and then the bell rang, and the passengers took their seats, and the train steamed out of the station, and plunged into the open country once again, routing up the gravel, and scattering stones and dust as it rushed along.

To heat and to dust there were, however, two travellers who seemed indifferent. Those two were Captain Stondon and his wife. After five years of moving from place to place, of seeing foreign countries, of living in hotels, in hired palaces, in Swiss châlets and French châteaux, they were returning by the 3·55 express to take up their head-quarters at Marshlands, and reside there for good.

With his back to the engine, with his hat off, with the warm breeze tossing his hair about and filling it full of dust, with his feet on the opposite seat, with the 'Times' lying beside him, Captain Stondon slept the sleep of the just, happily oblivious of the heat, and unconscious that Phemie was sitting in a direct draught.

She had taken off her bonnet, and drawn the blue silk curtain so as to shelter her eyes from the full glare of the sun, and while the train strained and throbbed along the rails, she looked out over the country through which they were passing.

Should you know her? Scarcely. The hair is the same that the summer sun shone down on in Tordale, but it is not the young hair that first entangled Captain Stondon's fancy. There is no part of us that ages like the hair. Look at a child's hair—a boy's—a man's. Watch the wind stirring each of them, and you will see what I mean. Every year as it passes by lays its hands on our heads, and takes something of freshness and of beauty from them. What is it? you ask. I do not know. But as we see that the leaves in August are not the same as they were in April, so we can perceive that the hair of a lad of nineteen is different from what it will be at four-and-twenty. It is young, like himself, at nineteen, and each year that comes and goes will make it, like himself, older.

Well, then, that glory of auburn hair had lost something of its beauty, or rather, perhaps, its beauty was different, just as Phemie's own loveliness was different.

She had been a girl then; she was a woman now—a woman in danger of becoming cold and worldly through mere prosperity and absence of trouble—a woman who disbelieved in broken hearts, in passionate love—who looked down from immeasureable heights of superiority on what she called boy and girl affection, and who thought of the dreams of her earlier life, when by chance they recurred to her memory, as she might of a foolish fairy tale, or of any other ridiculous fancy of her childish days.

A change had come over her! and Phemie acknowledged to herself that she was changed, as she looked out at the English scenery, which seemed so strange and unfamiliar to her eyes.

Through Middlesex, and Hertford, and Essex the train dashed on : the line passed first over the roofs of houses—over streets—over roads, and then the engine, settling into express-pace, sped away northward, beside the Lea, within sight of the prettily-wooded heights of Clapton, across the market-gardens at Tottenham, and so on, past Edmonton, and Waltham, and Broxbourne, and Elsenham to Audley End, through the grounds of which it dashed remorselessly, as though there was no park there people wanted to look at—no house they wished to see.

Then into the flat lands of Cambridgeshire, where each field seemed more level than the last, where willows grew in abundance, where the line ran beside swamps and osier beds, where there was nothing tall except the poplar trees, nothing to break the monotony of the scenery except church and cathedral towers.

After Cambridgeshire, Norfolk—great stretches of country, bare and bleak, that the fancy could roam out over as a man can take a walk : a country like Ireland, where you can dig peat and burn it, where you can walk miles without hedge or ditch or fence, where three hours from London you can imagine yourself at the world's end, from whence the express steamed rapidly on to the rich abbey-lands surrounding Wymondham.

And as she looked, she thought—thought of the five years that had come and gone—come and gone since she travelled from Wymondham to London before. Shall I tell you of her life, my reader, during those five years, before we go on to reach the end ?

To be a kind mistress, a faithful steward, to occupy herself in good works, to keep herself from vanity and idleness were, I think, all the admonitions Mr. Aggland gave his niece when he parted from her among the Cumberland mountains—excellent in their way, doubtless, but useless for the sufficient reason that Mrs. Stondon had no household to order, no wealth to squander, no opportunity of assisting others, no temptation to be over-proud either of her beauty or her position.

He might as well have told a man without a stomach to be careful of what he ate; but then Mr. Aggland had expected things to be different, and so, for that matter, had Phemie herself.

She thought that after the Scottish tour, after a few months on the Continent, she and her husband would return to Marshlands, and enter on that home life which is, I suppose, at some time or other, the temporal heaven of most women's imaginations.

She pictured to herself (in a vague, girlish way, of course,) the great rooms filled with company, the manner in which she would manage her establishment, the visits she would pay to the poor, the hours she would devote to study, and behold, as the dream hero and the dream future had faded out of her past life, so, when she was married, the dream of usefulness and the dream of a settled home faded more swiftly still, out of her present.

Captain Stondon did not much like England. Moreover, he desired that before his wife entered into English society she should combine every possible accomplishment, every grace of manner, every known knowledge of *les convenances* to her other charms.

As a matter of course, Phemie was ignorant of the world, ignorant of its usages, ignorant of what was expected from her as the mistress of Marshlands; and equally, perhaps, as a matter of course, Captain Stondon desired that she should become acquainted with the importance of her own position; with the world, with its usages, before he introduced her to society; and he was confirmed in this desire by Phemie's discomfiture at Montague Stondon's.

The girl was mountain bred, and had never been out to a party in her life.

Every man has his own idea of wisdom, and Captain Stondon's idea of the correct thing under the circumstances was to take his wife abroad, and keep her there.

In which idea he chanced to be wrong. Phemie

would have learned more of the conventionalities
of society in a week at home than she could possibly acquire during a twelvemonths' residence on
the Continent.

She was young enough to be moulded when he
married her; she was old enough to be a little
" eccentric " when she returned to England for
good.

Those who have been bred and brought up
in society, think, and think wrongly, that it is
a difficult matter for a willing pupil to acquire its
accent.

It lays such store by trifles, that it forgets what
trifles its usages really are, how soon they are
learnt.   It forgets that habit is second nature, and
that if habits can be formed early, they become
second nature itself.

Captain Stondon forgot this, at any rate, and
took Phemie abroad in consequence.

He had found a gem among the Cumberland
hills, and he wanted to have it ground and polished
before he presented it to English society.

He did not wish a speck to appear on its surface, a flaw to be even hinted at. The more valuable he perceived it to be, the more anxious he became that the world should not see it till no defect could he perceived, till no exception could be taken to the jewel he had discovered for himself, and discovering, had wed.

Captain Stondon, like most men who marry below their own station, desired that his wife should be educated late rather than never; but unlike the majority of his sex, his desires in this respect were fulfilled, not disappointed.

With the whole force and strength of her nature, Phemie devoted herself to learning. She had opportunities, and she embraced them; she had every advantage of masters that money could procure, and money never was better spent, than on so industrious and clever a pupil.

How she practised, how she studied, how she observed, no one ever knew fully except by the result.

Was it easy? It was like going to school after marriage; but nevertheless, with all her heart and with all her soul, Phemie tried to improve herself.

Was it happiness? Well, not exactly.· But, then, Phemie looked beyond the drudgery to the reward ; beyond the singing lessons to the time when she could show off her accomplishments in society. As the painter works for months in solitude, as the danseuse practises her most difficult steps for hours and days together, as the writer toils to finish his work, as the poet polishes and polishes his most musical lines, all for one end, one purpose—fame; so Phemie read, and studied, and laboured, that she might some day or other acquire social distinction.

Then she tired of it. Then suddenly, like a racer that has strained every nerve, and racked every muscle to reach the winning post—strained and racked beyond his strength—falls exhausted at last, a reaction set in. She wearied of travel, she wearied of hotels, she wearied of change of scene, wearied with an eternal longing, with a terrible heart-sickness for home.

It was nature asserting itself. It was the old time, the better time calling for her to come back ere she went too far ever to return; it was a passion, it was a fever; and through the long nights Phemie would lie awake and cry not the less bitterly, because silently, for home—for home!

When the southern sun was glaring down upon the earth, she thought of the mountain breezes, of the shady nooks among the hills, of the cool tarns, of the trickling streams. As a man in the first stage of fever dreams deliriously of gushing fountains, of flowing waters, so Phemie, with that home sickness on her, dreamt from morning till night about Tordale, about her own little room—her own no longer; about the heather, and the moss, and the ferns; about the clouds floating above Helbeck; about the mists enveloping Skillenscar.

Cumberland was rarely out of her mind; but when Cumberland faded away for a moment, it was only that Marshlands might take its place.

She had seen Marshlands, and whenever Tordale seemed too remote a spot to travel back to, whenever she wanted some nearer resting-place for her fancy to alight on, she folded her wings there, and wandered up and down under the elms and the fir-trees, through the gardens and the park, till she grew weary of imagining, and longed to start for England on the instant.

She did not like to say all that was in her heart about the matter. Captain Stondon had so evidently little intention of returning home that Phemie held her peace till she could refrain no longer.

Then, as is always the case with such natures, the stream burst its bounds all at once.

"Take me home, Henry, take me home, or I shall die," was her entreaty; and without a word of inquiry or remonstrance, Captain Stondon agreed that they should retrace their steps to England.

But they got no further than Paris. There the son Captain Stondon had been hoping for was born—dead. There the doctor said that if Phemie herself were to live, she must turn her face southward again; and with the old fever not cured, only subdued, Mrs. Stondon agreed to spend another winter abroad.

"Life was not worth having on the terms," she

told her physician; but then, as that individual remarked, only in politer terms than I can possibly translate—

" Her life was not quite her own to throw away for a mere whim. Her husband—" And that was enough for Phemie. She was very grateful to Captain Stondon; she would not have pained him for the world; she was very fond of him; she thought she loved him; she did more, she was sure she loved him, and so was everybody who saw them together. Her life was his, and for him she turned her back on England, and within sight of the promised land journeyed once again to the country, that was as a house of bondage unto her.

We have all felt home-sickness sometime or other; we have all hungered for the sea, or the hills, or the sun, or the bracing mountain breezes, with that mental hunger which is worse than any physical suffering; we have all wanted something in the course of our lives which we could not get; we have stretched out our hands unavailingly; we have sobbed through the darkness; we have pined, we have sickened; but the passion has ended at last, and we have sat down finally contented with our lot.

That was what Phemie did at any rate. She could not have continued fretting, and lived; but she ceased fretting and grew strong, and when, after all those years, she and her husband returned to England, there was no tumult in her breast about anything.

She had forgotten her dreams; she had almost forgotten her past; she had a kind and devoted husband; she had never repented her marriage; she had done well; she had made a very good and a very happy thing of life, and she was travelling down to Marshlands to take her proper place in society, with no breath of sorrow dimming the bright cold mirror of her existence.

Her sympathies had fallen to sleep with five years' want of exercise; her feelings had grown dull for very lack of sorrow; her intellect was expanded, her heart narrowed. Scenery itself was not to her now what it had once been; she looked on it as something which God had created for the benefit and amusement of the rich; she did not understand people being tempted; she did not comprehend people going wrong; a very shocking thing had happened in her husband's family—a thing which society never mentioned before him, and Phemie, of course, had been scandalised by it; but at the same time she could not comprehend how Montague Stondon could first forge another man's name, and then deliberately cut his own throat.

She had not liked Montague Stondon. He had placed her at a disadvantage; but it was shocking to think of a man committing suicide, and she felt very sorry for his wife and only son.

At the same time she was unable to understand why Captain Stondon took the matter so much to heart. He was not to blame. He had advanced money over and over again, till he grew weary of doing so, and if Mr. Montague Stondon liked to go and forge, how was her husband to know by intuition that he had done so?

Was he to blame for declining to send 1000*l.* to the barrister by return of post? He would have done it had his relative told him the scrape

he had got into, but he had not told him, and
Captain Stondon refused to make the advance,
and Montague Stondon cut his throat, and
Captain Stondon paid the money after all.

Phemie thought about Mr. Stondon's brown
eyes and elaborate whiskers and expensive dinner,
as the train swept through the flat lands surrounding Cambridge.

"How foolish they were to live beyond their
means!" thought this wise young woman, and
she would have said and thought the same about
any other sin or shortcoming. That her fellow-
creatures were but fallible; that flesh and blood
is prone to error; that to most the right is
difficult, the wrong easy; that the way to hell
is broad, that the path to heaven is narrow;—
these were things Phemie had yet to learn;
these were the realities she was travelling home
to meet; these were the lessons she had still to
con out of books she had never yet opened. Intellect, study, knowledge of all abstract sciences,
of what value are they if we remain ignorant of
the living volumes around us—if we have no com-

prehension of the struggles and temptations, of the sins and the sorrows, of the agony and the remorse, of the men and the women we meet day after day?

What shall we learn from Greek or from Roman, if the lines which have been traced by the hand of our God on the hearts of his creatures remain to us but as the writing on the wall? What shall it profit a man if he gain the whole world and lose his own soul? we are asked in the book which cannot speak foolishly—"if," as John Bunyan says, "the things of this world lie too close to his heart; if the earth with its things has bound up his roots; if he is an earth-bound soul wrapped up in thick clay?" And, in like manner, it is surely not too much to affirm that all knowledge and all power, all accomplishments, all grace, all wealth, are useless, are merely as sounding brass and as tinkling cymbals, unless there is joined to them a comprehension of the infirmities, temptations, sufferings of humanity.

To all, prosperity is a trial and a snare; but it is a worse trial and a worse snare to the young than to the old ; for which reason prosperity had not improved Mrs. Stondon. She had lived a purely selfish existence. "Fortune had placed a bandage over her eyes." Driving in a carriage through the pleasantest roads of this world, she took no thought of those who were limping along its roughest paths, its flintiest ways, foot-sore and weary. Fate had been so good to her, it had appointed her lot beside such cool streams, that she grew hard, and the Phemie who went out of England was not the Phemie who came back to it five years later.

And yet she was not changed quite past recognition. The old sweetness, the old truthfulness, the old frankness, the old steadiness of principle underlay the superstructure of selfishness and coldness which a too happy life had reared.

Beneath the world's burning suns, the flowers of her spring-time had withered away ; but the roots of the plants that had borne those flowers were still deep in her heart ready to bring forth leaves and buds and flowers again, and finally fruit if God saw fit ; and full though her existence might be of wealth and prosperity, still there was a vacant chamber which had never been unlocked by mortal hand, and which all the pomps and vanities, all the social successes, all the praises, all the popularity, all the flattery, and all the favour of this world would have been impotent to fill.

Sometimes when the twilight was stealing over the landscape—sometimes when the fleecy clouds chased each other across the sky—when she sat looking up at the great mountains, or from among myrtle bowers gazed out over the sea—sometimes when she remained very still and very quiet—when the rush of many feet was silent, when the sound of merriment died away, when she was alone with herself, alone with her lonely life, with her empty heart—I think she must have felt that there was a want in her existence—that she had somehow missed the mark—that God never intended the Phemie Keller who had danced across the hills to Strammer Tarn, who had nursed the children at the farm, who had cried if a person only looked crossly at her, who had been loved and cared for, who had been in

such trouble at leaving the old home faces behind her, to develop into Phemie Stondon, who,
without a pulse throbbing faster at the antici-
pation, was travelling home to Marshlands to
perform the duties of her station, or to neglect
them, as matters should turn out.

Nevertheless, she was glad to get back to
England. The idea of a settled abode was pleasant to her; she wanted to see her uncle, and
Helen, and Duncan; she thought, with society,
that she and Captain Stondon had stayed away
from their duties long enough; she quite believed
that country gentlemen ought to reside for some
portion of the year, at all events, on their pro-
perties; and further, she was tired of the Continent, tired of the heat, tired of the sun, tired of
foreign languages, of strange tongues, of resi-
dences which were not homes.

There was another reason why Phemie desired
to settle in England : she was tired of having
Captain Stondon constantly at her elbow; but
this, of course, was not the way she put it to
herself.

He had those duties to perform I have made mention of before, and he ought to return to fulfil them. A man of property had scarcely a right to spend year after year in climbing mountains, in looking at old ruins, in making foreign friends, in spending money abroad. Phemie quite thought he ought to take up his abode at Marshlands, and was very glad when he said that he agreed with her.

Montague Stondon's death had been a shock to him. It reminded him of purposes unaccomplished in his own life, of negligence, nfaithfulness, of good resolutions forgotten, of good intentions unfulfilled. He would return and do better for the future; and accordingly he returned, and, unmindful of heat and dust, slept on till the train reached Disley.

It was evening then, and while the carriage which met them at Disley rolled along the level sandy roads, Phemie looked eagerly and longingly for the woods surrounding Marshlands. She strained her eyes for them as she had not strained them to catch a first sight of famous cities far away, and yet when she beheld the firs and the elms reflected against the sky, when she saw the trees lifting their heads to heaven, when she caught the sunset glory bathing the whole scene in a flood of crimson light, an indefinable feeling of sadness came over her, and her heart grew heavy to remember that the landscape and the woods were the same as they had been when she looked upon them soon after her marriage, but that she was changed—that she was going back another Phemie from the Phemie her husband had married, to her husband's house.

END OF VOL. I.

BRADBURY, EVANS, AND CO., PRINTERS, WHITEFRIARS.

TINSLEY BROTHERS' NEW WORKS.

TEN YEARS IN SARÁWAK. By CHARLES
BROOKE, the Tuan-Mudah of Saráwak. With an Introduction by
H.H. the Rajah SIR JAMES BROOKE, and numerous Illustrations.
Uniform with Captain Burton's "Mission to Dahomey." In 2 vols.
[*Ready.*

THE HISTORY OF FRANCE under the BOUR-
BONS. By CHARLES DUKE YONGE, Author of "The History of
the Royal Navy." In 2 vols. 8vo. [*Ready.*

THE REGENCY OF ANNE OF AUSTRIA, Queen
of France, Mother of Louis XIV. From Published and Unpublished
Sources. By Miss FREER, Author of "The Married Life of Anne of
Austria." In 2 vols. 8vo. [*Shortly.*

A TRIP TO BARBARY BY A ROUNDABOUT
ROUTE. By GEORGE AUGUSTUS SALA. In 1 vol.
[*Ready this day.*

MODERN CHARACTERISTICS : A Series of Essays
from the *Saturday Review*, revised by the Author. In 1 vol. haud-
somely printed, and bevelled boards. [*Ready.*

CONTENTS :

1. False Steps.	16. Friendly Infatuation.
2. The Uses of Dignity.	17. Pithiness.
3. Quarrels.	18. The Theory of Life from Below
4. Social Salamanders.	Stairs.
5. Vague Aims.	19. Needy Men.
6. Falling Off.	20. Philosophers and Politicians.
7. Minor Tribulations.	21. Authors and Books.
8. Thrift.	22. Literary Industry.
9. Domestic Autocracy.	23. Nineteenth Century Sadness.
10. Culpability and Degradation.	24. Weakness of Public Opinion.
11. Husbands.	25. Pagan Patriotism.
12. The Companions of our Pleasures.	26. Occasional Cynicism.
13. Clever Men's Wives.	27. Praise and Blame.
14. New Ideas.	28. The Artisan and his Friends.
15. Cynical Fallacies.	29. The Terrors of Intellect.

LIFE OF GEORGE THE THIRD : from Published
and Unpublished Sources. By J. HENEAGE JESSE, Esq. In
3 vols. 8vo. [*Shortly.*

BIOGRAPHIES OF CELEBRATED MEN and
WOMEN. By ALPHONSE DE LAMARTINE. In 2 vols. [*Shortly.*

NEW EDITION, REVISED, OF EVERYDAY PAPERS.

EVERYDAY PAPERS. Reprinted from " All the Year Round," and adapted for Evening Readings at Mechanics' Institutes, Penny Reading Clubs, &c. By ANDREW HALLIDAY. In 1 vol.

ST. MARTIN'S EVE. By Mrs. H. WOOD, Author of " East Lynne," &c. In 3 vols. [*Ready.*

PHEMIE KELLER. By the Author of " George Geith," "Maxwell Drewitt," &c. In 3 vols. [*Ready.*

MAXWELL DREWITT: A Novel. By the Author of " George Geith," " City and Suburb." In 3 vols. [*Ready this day.*

SANS MERCI. By the Author of " Guy Livingstone." &c. In 3 vols. [*Ready.*

CARLETON GRANGE: A Novel. By the Author of " Abbot's Cleve." In 3 vols. [*Ready.*

RUNNING THE GAUNTLET: A Novel. By EDMUND YATES, Author of " Broken to Harness," &c. In 3 vols. [*Ready.*

WHAT MONEY CAN'T DO: A Novel. By the Author of " Altogether Wrong." In 3 vols. [*Ready.*

HALF-A-MILLION OF MONEY: A Novel. By AMELIA B. EDWARDS, Author of " Barbara's History." In 3 vols. [*Ready.*

RHODA FLEMING: A Novel. By GEORGE MEREDITH, Author of " The Ordeal of Richard Feverell," &c. In 3 vols. [*Ready.*

MISS FORESTER: A Novel. By Mrs. EDWARDS, Author of " The Morals of Mayfair," &c. In 3 vols. [*Ready.*

THE OLD LEDGER: A Novel. By G. L. M. STRAUSS. In 3 vols. [*Ready.*

JOHN NEVILLE; Soldier, Sportsman, and Gentleman : A Novel. By Captain NEWALL. In 2 vols. [*Ready.*

EMILY FOINDER: A new Novel. In 3 vols. By F. DEVONSHIRE. [*Ready.*

TINSLEY BROTHERS, 18, CATHERINE STREET, STRAND.